# THE CASTLE ROSE

# THE CASTLE ROSE

TABITHA CAPLINGER

BLUE INK
PRESS

ISBN: 9781948449236

Library of Congress Control Number: 2024941590

Cover by Laura Hollingsworth

Published in the United States by Blue Ink Press, LLC

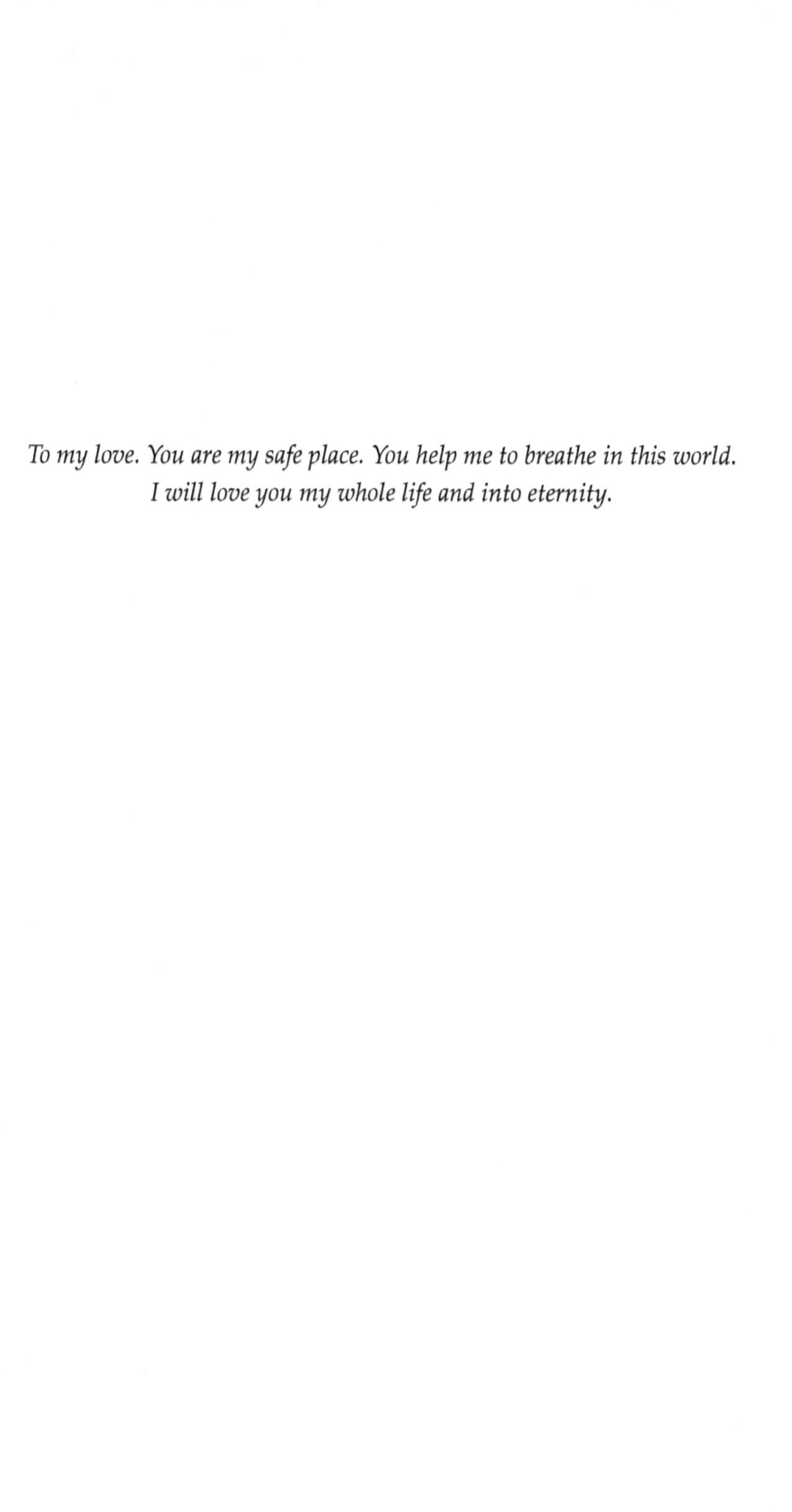

*To my love. You are my safe place. You help me to breathe in this world. I will love you my whole life and into eternity.*

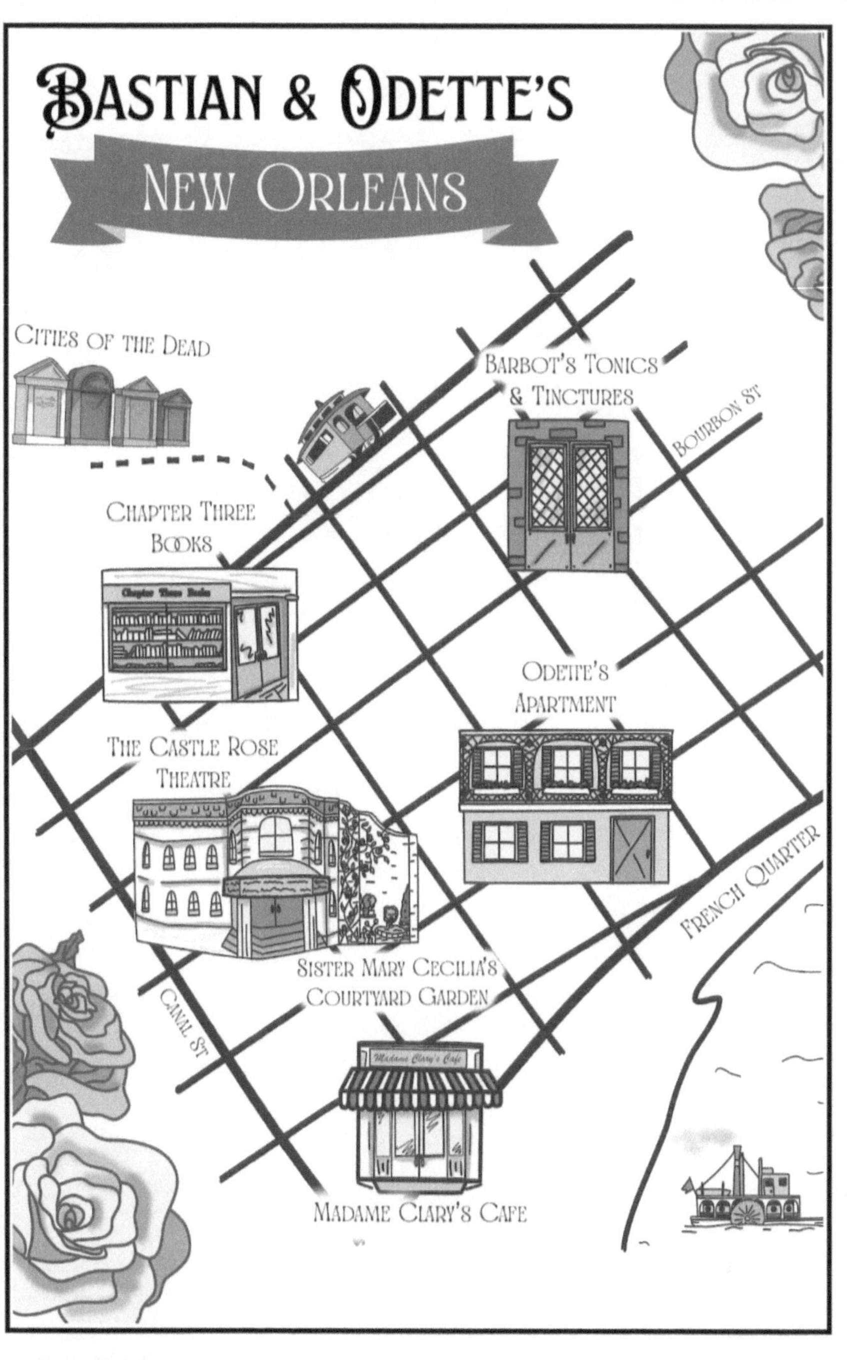

BASTIAN & ODETTE'S
NEW ORLEANS
CITIES OF THE DEAD
BARBOT'S TONICS & TINCTURES
BOURBON ST
CHAPTER THREE BOOKS
Chapter Three Books
ODETTE'S APARTMENT
THE CASTLE ROSE THEATRE
FRENCH QUARTER
SISTER MARY CECILIA'S COURTYARD GARDEN
CANAL ST
Madame Clary's Cafe
MADAME CLARY'S CAFE

# PRELUDE: OCTAVIAN ZANE, 1923

ome seemed a strange word to describe New Orleans. Octavian Zane wore it like new shoes; tight and a little ill-fitting until they had been broken in. He leaned against the bar and sipped from a dingy glass, watching the jovial faces of patrons as they clapped and gyrated to the jazz bleeding from the stage. The crowd moved in the illusion of freedom while the very air strangled him. He loosened his tie and took another swig of his bitter drink.

"You look positively grummy." A smooth voice and a soft slap against his shoulder interrupted his simmering thoughts.

Catherine was all dolled up in a cotton lace dress with shimmering beads in a deep green that accentuated her eyes. She primped her brunette curls as she sat on the stool next to him.

Octavian gestured for the bartender, Bert, to give the lady a drink. "You know me, Cat. I like to play up the suffering artist bit."

She held her cocktail with dainty fingers. "Someone is going to come along and think you are a genius with oils and canvas." She took a sip. "I just know it."

She winked at him and offered a sweet smile filled with her incessant optimism that he wasn't sure if he loved or hated. He had learned, in their short acquaintance, that it was useless to argue with her because Catherine held an aversion to anything melancholy or any lack of hope for the future. She had also never starved for anything; had never been beaten down and broken along the way.

Applause erupted. Catherine giggled and clapped her own hands.

Bastian Roux, the club's headliner, stood from his piano, took a bow then hopped off the stage. He meandered through the crowd with a shy smile as patrons patted him on the back or shook his hand while offering praise for his performance.

Octavian tried to rub away the low throb behind his eyes.

"I need water, Bert." Bastian breathed heavily as he stepped up to the bar beside Octavian and Catherine. Sweat dripped from his forehead and the ends of his messy hair.

"That was a great set," Catherine cooed, placing a diamond-adorned hand on the pianist's chest. "I just loved that last song."

"How could it not be great with my muse in the audience?" Bastian kissed her jaw, then nuzzled his nose against her neck.

Octavian avoided gagging by swallowing the last of his whiskey. He held up the empty glass so the bartender would pour him another round. "They do love you," Octavian murmured. The crowd, Catherine, heck, all of New Orleans seemed to love Bastian. They flocked to The Castle Rose, or any speakeasy in the city that found him behind the piano. "Thanks for giving my name to the doorman or I might not have gotten in tonight." He drank down his refill in one swallow.

Bastian patted him on the back. "Of course. That's what friends are for," he said, and Octavian watched as he turned the gold signet ring on his finger so that the embossed rose aligned with his knuckle. Then Bastian chugged half his glass of water, wiped his mouth with his thumb, and kissed Catherine's cheek. "I've got another set in just a few minutes. I better go get ready."

Catherine's entire countenance lit up as she watched her

fiancé retreat backstage. Octavian dimmed, sinking heavily onto his barstool.

*That's what friends are for.* Ha! Octavian held his empty glass to the bartender again, watching as it was filled with amber liquid.

From the outside looking in, one might assume he and Bastian were the same—young, artistic transplants finding a new life in the Big Easy. But age and relocation were all they had in common. While Bastian talked of leaving his mother behind with fond homesickness that even the distance of an entire ocean could not fade, Octavian desired only to forget the impoverished parents who had abandoned him to be little more than a farm-hand for strangers who had wanted to be called family. While he would not call Bastian spoiled, he had watched the musical prodigy get handed everything he himself wanted. Yet Octavian couldn't even beg, borrow, or steal to get ahead.

The stage lights illuminated the waiting instruments as the band stepped out. A few bass strings were plucked. Bastian tickled out a handful of notes. The crowd whooped and cheered. Catherine squealed and giggled. She waved a few fingers at her beau, who returned the gesture with a wink and a grin before unleashing the magic of his God-given talent on his waiting audience. Octavian swilled the contents of his glass, which dulled his senses as it burned its way through his hollow places.

"You still here?" Bastian plopped down on the barstool next to Octavian.

The Castle Rose had long emptied, aside from waiters wiping down tables and the bartender drying and shelving glasses. The stage lights had been off for at least an hour as Octavian had stewed in his scheming, wondering if there was a magic in this mystic city that could give him all he wanted.

Octavian checked the time on the pocket watch he had stolen as a teenager in St. Louis. "I got caught up daydreaming, I guess." Octavian slid his empty glass to the barkeep. "Probably had one too many tonight. What brings you back in? I thought you were walking Catherine home?"

"I did, but it's too late for any kind of invitation inside. Her mother wouldn't allow it. Besides, she's got church in the morning. But I'm going to meet her for lunch after." Bastian spun his charcoal gray newsboy flat cap on his finger. "Popped in to grab my lucky hat."

"Maybe that's what I'm missing. A lucky hat." Octavian snatched the wool tam from Bastian's hands.

Bastian laughed. "You can have it if you think it'll help. I'm happy to share my luck with a friend."

"Are we friends?" The question slipped out before Octavian could stifle it.

"Of course we are!" Bastian slung his arm around Octavian's shoulder and squeezed. "We've both left families behind in the adventurous pursuit of our dreams. Perhaps fate would make us brothers."

Brothers would not have been the word Octavian would have chosen. Not even friends. Rivals at best. But before he could decide if he was flattered or appalled at the sentiment, Bastian began to cough; a tickle in his throat morphed into hacks and wheezes. He pulled a handkerchief from his pocket and covered his mouth as he continued to gasp.

"Need some water?" Octavian asked.

Bastian dismissed the offer with a quick shake of his head. He seemed to finally catch his breath, inhaling with a deep rasp. When he lowered his hand, the white linen rag held the faintest tinge of pink.

Was Bastian mortal, after all?

"Are you okay?" Octavian asked.

"Yeah." Bastian wiped a reddish drip from his mouth. "I've just been feeling a little under the weather lately. Nothing that a restful Sunday won't cure."

"If you say so." Octavian returned Bastian's hat, feeling like maybe it wasn't all that lucky after all. Perhaps the powers-that-be did not adore the young musician as much as Octavian had once thought.

"I do," Bastian said. He patted Octavian on the back as he stood up. "You should join us for lunch tomorrow. Catherine's mother makes the best fried chicken, I swear."

"Maybe," Octavian replied.

He watched Bastian exit behind the dark stage. The rest of the house lights clicked off. The barkeep gestured to his watch, and Octavian got the hint. He ran a hand through his black hair as he started to leave. A phantom wind whipped by, chilling the back of his neck.

# CHAPTER I
# BASTIAN, 2024

astian Roux made it his habit to ride the trolley every morning. Mingled amongst the tourists and locals—trapped between living and dying—he took a daily trip from the French Quarter to the Cities of the Dead and back again. Mostly he stood. Occasionally, he sat until another rider forced him to move to avoid being sat upon. Always he looked out the windows into the world which he could only partly touch, a world that had long forgotten him, a world he both missed and despised.

This morning was a bit rainy. Not enough to stop him from walking down the street. It was the kind of thin mist which stuck to you in such a way you didn't even realize you had gotten wet until you were back indoors. Not that he could feel the rain anymore. But he remembered what it felt like. Just like he remembered the sweet taste of freshly made beignets. As the trolley passed a cafe, he smelled the fried dough, and his tongue tricked him into thinking powdered sugar was dissolving into sweet syrup in his mouth. He wiped a finger over his lips.

The bell dinged, and the trolley slowed to a stop, making Bastian lurch forward just a bit. His eyes perused the faces on the sidewalk. Several of them were familiar. Faces he saw every day.

Faces of his neighbors, not that they would recognize his. There was a new face, though. It was smooth ivory with delicate features, light pink lips, and even lighter pink cheeks framed by long, soft waves that were somewhere between blonde and brown without really being either. Her eyes were just as indistinguishable. As the light danced in them, they wavered from gray to green to brown, always sparkling…and staring straight at him.

Could she see him?

Someone bumped into her, and she looked away, tucking a strand of hair behind her ear, and pushing her glasses up on her nose. Bastian sighed. He ran his fingers through his own short, messy curls. It must have been a mirage. Another illusion his tired mind was using to keep him from succumbing totally to the darkness of his despair.

He glanced at the street once more. She was still there, fixing the button on her dark green cardigan. She adjusted the bag on her shoulder and raised her gaze back toward the trolley. As the streetcar pulled away, Bastian's eyes locked with hers again, and she smiled. Could the impossible have just become possible? No. A hundred years of this curse made him no less of a fool. It was a trick, like the sugar. She couldn't have seen him. He could not be seen.

# CHAPTER 2
# ODETTE

Odette Durand didn't notice the magic at play behind the scenes of her first day in New Orleans. To be fair, she hadn't had coffee yet, and the lack of caffeine meant her brain cells were still half asleep at best. Walking through the foggy, misty morning, the newness of a grand and vibrant city she now called home blurred around her. It overwhelmed her senses. This was to be her grand adventure. A sweeping change she hoped would bring fresh inspiration and heal her bruised heart.

Six months ago, her fiancé had broken up with her.

She had been devastated at first. But it wasn't so much about grieving the loss of him as much as it had been grieving the loss of the life she had imagined and planned for. The one where she married a good guy, had a nice house, eventually a couple of kids, and felt safe. Then again, she'd always thought safe was a tad overrated.

But thinking that and living it out were two different beasts.

She had packed up and moved because she'd refused to live small. People might say it was so she wouldn't have to bump into him at the supermarket or church, but it wasn't. His departure from their planned future was sudden and upsetting, but after a few days of binge-watching and crying into a pint of Rocky Road, the shock wore off, and the anger set in.

How dare he ask her to marry him and then just take it back.

An evening with her older sisters, who'd hosted a boyfriend-bonfire in his honor, had helped Odette realize that she didn't want to marry him, anyway. Roasting marshmallows over the flaming mementos of her failed relationship had brought a certain closure and clarity. He had never seen *her*—she had not really seen him—and at the core, didn't everyone just want to be truly seen?

Life held more for Odette. At least she hoped it did. Her parents were the type of people who had raised her to believe she was meant for greatness. She wasn't exactly sure what that entailed. *Greatness* often felt heavy; too heavy for the likes of her. Somewhere along the way, it had become so heavy that she'd put it down and settled for that safe dream, which had ended up being not so dependable either. She'd found herself pushing thirty and no closer to greatness than she had been at fifteen or twenty. She wasn't even really sure that she was meant for great-ness, but she was sure she needed wide open spaces to try and breathe and fail and feel. She needed to take a risk, or perhaps she would never see herself.

There were no risks in her small town in Virginia, so she had widened her search parameters and found a job managing a small bookshop in the Crescent City. Loading all her life in boxes and into a moving van terrified her.

*"It's not brave if you're not scared."*

That was a line from a movie she'd watched once, one that she'd repeated to herself often, and which motivated her just enough to push her forward. Pulling away from her tiny town-house, she'd looked in the rearview mirror at her parents and sisters waving. She'd cried for the first two hours of the drive. The further she got from home, the less safe she'd felt, but also the more she knew it was the right move. Something in her marrow whispered to her a steady confirmation. It was the divine voice she trusted more than her fear.

It whispered to her this morning as she meandered down the uncharted sidewalks, making herself a mental map and looking for a cafe. She detected a whiff of brew and baked goods before she saw the sign. Madame Clary's Cafe was just on the other side of the trolley stop. Navigating the crowd that waited for the coming streetcar was a bit of a nuisance. Did no one understand how much she needed a latte this morning?

Odette tried to dodge and weave her way between the tourists and businessmen but didn't have much luck. It was a test of patience, and she was failing. But her mother taught her to never be rude, so she chose to just wait for the walkway to clear once the trolley moved on its way. She bided her time by taking in the scenery of the street. Either side was lined with brick buildings and iron-trimmed balconies. There were spots of color and greenery that made it feel alive. However, something haunting mingled within. Maybe it was the age of the architecture or the weather—but it lurked—a bit of darkness below the surface.

The trolley bell rang and Odette shivered. Through the window of the stopping streetcar, she saw a man about her age. She wasn't sure if it was reflections in the glass or a trick of the light, but he almost seemed to fade into the background, which she supposed was what drew her eye to him. His ginger-brown curls were unruly. His face was pallid and thin, framed by his high cheekbones. His lips were pursed, and his blue eyes looked…sad.

What could make someone look so lost?

He saw her. She probably shouldn't stare. Her mother would not approve of her analyzing glare. Another man bumped into her as he passed by to get on the trolley, causing her bag to slip from her shoulder and pulling her sweater and her attention. She regained her composure and then looked back at the man on the trolley. She offered him a smile, a gesture of kindness to brighten whatever shadows were clouding his day. The streetcar pulled away, and she returned to her quest for coffee.

Once completed, Odette sipped her hot mocha on her way back to her new apartment. She didn't give a second thought to the man she had seen on the trolley or to the soft music she now heard wafting through the warm air from some unknown origin along the street. She let the sorrow in each note float over her head, just barely kissing her ears before fading into the buzz of the morning.

# CHAPTER 3
# ODETTE

Odette's toothbrush dangled from her mouth. Her bare toes wiggled on the chilly black and white tile floor and her hands rested on the edge of the pedestal sink as she leaned forward to get a good look at her reflection in the bathroom mirror. She didn't look as tired as she felt, but a couple more nights of being afraid of the shadows in the corners of her bedroom might change that. When had she reverted back to her childhood days of being scared of the dark? It was silly. She knew that. Nothing was hiding behind the curtains—nothing was waiting to jump out of the closet. Her door had three very secure locks because her father had told her three times to make that the first thing she took care of when she'd arrived. He'd even bought her new screws and an extra deadbolt.

Maybe it was just the new place. Everything felt unfamiliar. Even the smell of her apartment—a mix of must and old cigars— it wasn't home yet. She made a mental note to get cleaner and candles on her way home from work.

Work. Today was her first day at the bookshop. Any place where she could be surrounded by quiet and books would feel like home, and the shop owner sounded so sweet every time they talked on the phone that Odette didn't have much anxiety about this part of her adventure. Her only real concern was what to wear. She ran through outfit choices in her mind while she finished brushing her teeth, washing her face, and combing her wavy hair. Hepburn, her petite black cat, rubbed against her leg.

"Are you an Audrey this morning or a Katharine? Will you be sweetness or spunk?" Odette scratched the cat between her ears, and it purred.

Hepburn meowed a reply, then pranced from the room.

Odette followed her pet out of the bathroom, stepping into the small bedroom. From her closet, she retrieved a pair of skinny jeans and a black peplum blouse with matching pearlescent buttons and lace trim. She dressed, finishing the outfit with her favorite long, gold tassel necklace and her grandmother's turquoise ring. She grabbed her black flats and pulled them on as she shuffled to the kitchenette.

Her apartment was tiny, but it was also perfect, with exposed brick and the charm of a different era. It would be even more perfect when she finished unpacking her last few boxes. Thankfully, she had been sure to set up her very important coffee maker the night before in preparation for this morning. She filled it with water and searched through the cabinets to find the bag of ground coffee. It felt too light. She whispered a small prayer for provision, a plea that her fears were not about to come true, but it was of no use. Odette opened the bag to find there were mere crumbs left—only a few measly grounds—not nearly enough for a tablespoon of coffee, much less a whole cup.

"How did this happen? How could I not triple-check?" Odette whined mostly to herself, but also to Hepburn, who jumped onto the counter and sauntered toward her like a very tiny panther.

"Hepburn, there's no coffee. What has become of me, of my life? I've lost all control, all direction. I'm wavering, dear cat, wavering!"

Hepburn meowed.

"You're right. That was a bit melodramatic," Odette replied.

"There's no need to panic. That sweet cafe is still just a stroll away and not far from the bookstore. All will be well." She picked up the cat, kissed its head, then set it on the floor.

Odette made sure Hepburn had food and water for the day before offering her faithful companion a goodbye as she grabbed her purse and headed out the door and toward coffee. Another morning with a mocha wouldn't be the worst thing.

Odette was still getting her bearings in New Orleans. She needed to pay close attention to where she was headed and not too much on the surrounding beauty. Some of it was hard to miss and harder to ignore. Like the red roses that climbed up the side of an abandoned building. Or the sad music, the melody she recognized from the previous morning, returning to her senses, leaving a deeper impression. It sounded tragically beautiful. Where did it come from? Music was everywhere in this city, but mostly it was a happier jazz. This was different, and it pricked at her heart. Then it just stopped, disappeared from her ears like a phantom she wasn't even sure had ever been real.

Waxing poetic meant Odette most definitely needed coffee. When she finally arrived at Madame Clary's Café, there was already a line out the door. Not that it was that long—the cafe was relatively small, but still. It was another obstacle to being caffeinated. She did her best to remain patient as she inched her way from the sidewalk to the door, and eventually to the counter.

"Well, good mornin', doll," the dark-haired, dark-skinned woman behind the counter crooned. "You were in here yesterday. Have I managed to get myself another regular?" She smiled wide. "You must be new in the Big Easy, or at least over here in the Quarter, because I pride myself on knowing everyone… keeps a small-town feel."

"Yes, I'm brand new," Odette responded. "You must be Madame Clary."

"Heavens no!" The woman threw her head back and laughed. The motion made her large earrings dangle and dance. "If there ever was an actual Madame Clary, she was about three or four owners ago. I'm Elizabeth, most call me Lizzie though." She wiped her hand on her white apron and then reached over the counter.

"I'm Odette Durand." She accepted the offered handshake. "I'm the new manager at Chapter Three Books."

"Well, Odette, the new manager," Lizzie replied. "What can I get for you?"

"Just a large mocha," Odette answered.

"No pastry?" The woman's bright demeanor momentarily drooped, and she put a hand on her round, cocked hip. "Nonsense, I'm giving you a couple of beignets. You need some carbs to get you through 'til lunchtime."

"You don't have to…"

"Consider it a welcome to the Quarter gift," Lizzie patted Odette's hand. "Besides, my beignets are the best in the city no matter what the tourist websites say… Joe, grab a couple of the freshest beignets for our new friend Odette here," Lizzie called over her shoulder then grinned at Odette again. "They'll be just a minute."

"Thank you." Odette stepped to the side out of line and out of the way so the next person could order. She really didn't care much about fancy doughnuts and would have rather just gotten her latte and been on her way to work, but this was the first person, besides her landlord, she had spoken to since arriving. Meeting new people wasn't easy for Odette, but Lizzie seemed nice and warm, and a little nice warmth could go a long way in making her feel a little more at home here.

"So, how do you like our fair city so far?" Lizzie asked between customers.

"It's quite beautiful," Odette began as she grabbed her hot mocha from the barista. "A bit haunting." She took a cautious sip. "Like the mist and fog yesterday, and the sad music I heard passing that old theater on my walk over."

"The music, eh?" Lizzie raised an eyebrow and chuckled. "That's one I haven't heard in a while."

"What do you mean?"

"This city is full of ghost stories and the haunted theater used to be a favorite when I first took over this cafe, but not so much anymore." Lizzie took another order.

"Haunted theater?" Odette didn't believe in ghosts, but a good story always intrigued her.

"Story goes that about a hundred years ago, a musician, pretty popular for the time…" Lizzie handed off a coffee and a muffin to another customer in line. "Well, things get twisted; maybe he was cursed, maybe he was murdered by a jealous rival, or maybe he died of a broken heart when his sweetheart ran off with another man." She leaned her elbows on the counter near Odette. "Point is, he died, and they say his ghost haunts the old theater where he used to perform. They say if you listen closely, you can still hear him play the piano while he waits for his true love to return…or some such thing."

"True love?" Odette laughed.

"Not the romantic, I see?" Lizzie was handed a small brown paper bag, and she passed it along to Odette. "Careful. If you heard the music, you might be that true love." Lizzie winked and then laughed out loud.

Odette shivered and then giggled. "Poor guy will spend eternity alone then."

Lizzie laughed again, a belly laugh that shook her shoulders and made her brown eyes water. "I like you, Odette Durand. If you don't like the romance angle, Sister Mary Cecilia might have a different theory about the music. The abbey's next door to the theater and she's usually out there tending her garden and those roses growing up the wall. You could always ask for her take on it all."

Odette just nodded. She didn't care enough about old ghost stories to engage in more conversation with complete strangers.

This interaction was already testing the bounds of her introversion.

"Well, enjoy those beignets, darlin'," Lizzie said.

"Thank you. I will." Odette waved and then left.

When she got outside, she opened the bag and inhaled the aroma of fried oil and sugar. Her stomach growled, and she relented to its command. The beignet was still warm. She shook a bit of the powdered sugar off so that it wouldn't leave a trail of dust on her blouse and took a large bite. It almost melted in her mouth. She licked the sugar residue from her lips.

She had never had a beignet before, so while she had nothing to compare it to, Odette had a hard time believing there could be a better one out there. She stuffed the rest of the fried dough in her mouth, took a sip of her mocha to wash it down, and headed to the bookshop.

Somewhere behind her, the music played again, a faint tickle that barely penetrated her thoughts. She considered Lizzie's story, imagining a lonely and lovelorn ghost. For a split second, she felt sorry for him before she came to her senses and remembered there was no such thing as ghosts.

# CHAPTER 4
# ODETTE

Odette stepped inside the pine green door of Chapter Three Books for the first time and was hit by the smell of its waiting tomes. Vintage lights that hung from brass chains cast a warm glow over the space. Every wall was lined, floor to ceiling, with dark oak shelves, and each shelf was packed with books. More shelves and a mishmash of tables used for display filled the center of the shop.

"Good morning! You must be Odette!" An older woman rushed out from behind the forest green-painted counter. A maroon scarf was wrapped around silver hair. She wore a denim shirt and several beaded necklaces and bracelets in a variety of colors. Thick, tortoiseshell frames adorned her face. She reached out her hand.

"Yes, and you must be Isabelle," Odette said, taking her hand and returning the greeting. She hoped her palms weren't too clammy.

The handshake turned into a hug. "I'm so glad you are here!" Isabelle released Odette. "Did you get settled into your apartment okay? Do you need anything? Where should we start this morning?" Isabelle, the owner of the bookstore, returned to the counter, leaning over it with a hand under her chin and no apparent intention of letting Odette actually answer one of her questions.

Odette laughed and followed.

"You can put your bag here." The shop owner pointed to a cubby under the cash register.

Odette obeyed, then spied the board hanging on the wall behind the counter. It was covered in photos, postcards, and newspaper clippings. Everything from a few best-selling authors signing books to children's parties and even an eight-by-ten image of a younger Isabelle in a ball gown holding a feathered mask with *"Masquerade, 1997"* scribbled along the bottom.

"It was a wondrous evening," Isabelle sighed at the same image. "That is our memory board," she said. "We are always adding to it, so we don't forget all the good and fun we've had."

"I love that," Odette replied.

A smile curved the woman's bright, pink-stained lips. "Now, let's introduce you to the shop, shall we?"

"Yes," Odette nodded, ready to take mental notes of all the pertinent information about her new job.

Isabelle had needed help for quite some time, so the rest of Odette's first day became a quick course in their procedures before taking care of stocking and organizing the messy, unattended shelves that lined the walls of the small shop. She took a break to sit in on story time with the preschoolers, who wiggled and giggled on the faded area rug at the back of the store as Isabelle read them a fairytale.

At three in the afternoon, they stopped to enjoy a cup of tea. Isabelle said taking tea together was an unbreakable tradition necessary for shop morale. Odette didn't argue. She enjoyed sitting in the cozy tufted chairs by the large front window and chatting about books, the city, and life with the gray-haired, bright-eyed woman. Isabelle had traveled the world in her youth. Her younger years were full of adventure and romance and, if the fraction she shared over this first cup of tea was any indication, Odette was going to greatly enjoy plumbing the depths of the older woman's history.

When their cups were empty, Isabelle jumped back into action, bustling around the shop. She was a wrinkled bundle of energy. A bohemian, a free spirit with a smile that expressed the true joy of a life well lived and well loved. She chatted with customers, leading them from shelf to shelf in search of the perfect book—a search which left piles on the floor and side tables, and provided Odette with an explanation for how the little shop got so out of sorts. Following behind Isabelle to keep the place organized would be a full-time job in and of itself.

Not that Odette minded. She had already fallen in love with this place and its smell of old pages and scented candles. It felt cozy and inviting. The kind of place you wanted to retreat to on a rainy day. The kind of place you could get lost in for hours, strolling amongst the shelves or curled up in a chair reading a new volume.

"I think that is enough for today, my dear." Isabelle reached over Odette's shoulder and took the books she was sorting out of her hand.

"It's only 5:30? We don't close for another half hour," Odette protested.

"I think you've more than earned your keep cleaning up after me today." Isabelle took Odette by the hand and gently pulled her toward the front desk. "And I'm sure you're still getting settled in your new apartment. So…" She handed Odette her purse, "…listen to a nice old lady and take off a little early. This will all still be here tomorrow."

Odette sighed. "I wouldn't want to argue with—"

"You certainly wouldn't. You wouldn't win." Isabelle winked.

"I do need to run to the market, so I guess I'll see you in the morning." Odette took off her reading glasses and tucked them into her bag.

"See you bright and early," Isabelle called over her shoulder, already scurrying back into the small maze of shelves.

Odette laughed to herself and opened the front door. The little bell that hung from the top of the door rang, signaling her exit onto the street. The sky dimmed as the sun started its descent. The diner across the street smoked BBQ in the alleyway, and the spicy aroma made Odette's stomach growl. But she was on a budget until payday so no eating out. She would go to the market and then go home to cook her dinner.

Less than an hour later, Odette walked back down the street with a beige shopping bag in one hand and her purse in the other. Turning the corner, the saxophone music from two blocks away faded into the tragic piano from the morning.

Was she going crazy?

Lizzie's ghost story waltzed around in her head to the slow beat of the haunting tune. Was she hearing anything at all or was this some stress-induced figment of her imagination?

Passing the faded brick and dilapidated windows of the abandoned theater, Odette saw a figure pruning the rose bush that climbed its way up the wall. She was short and old, with deep wrinkles and plump cheeks, and wore the tunic and habit of a nun. As she clipped thorny vines, she swayed and hummed, seemingly to the same melody filling Odette's senses.

Odette approached the iron gate that led into the courtyard which connected the theater and the abbey.

"Oh hello, dear." The sister smiled. She removed her gardening gloves as she stepped closer to Odette. "Please do come in."

"Oh, I didn't want to intrude, I just..." Odette's heart raced. What was she doing? Was she going to ask a stranger about imaginary music? Was it imaginary? It all felt too ridiculous, and Odette could not bring herself to have this peculiar conversation.

"There is no such thing as an intrusion around here." The old woman opened the gate, waiting for Odette to step inside.

"I'm sorry. I-I just wanted to tell you the roses are lovely," Odette stammered.

The nun raised an eyebrow. "Thank you."

Before any more could be asked or spoken, Odette dipped her head in an awkward nod and hustled away down the sidewalk. She heard the gate creak closed and scolded herself for being rude and weird.

At home, Odette sautéed vegetables and boiled pasta for her dinner for one. Hepburn purred and rubbed against her leg. "My day was fine," Odette said to the cat.

Hepburn meowed and hopped onto the counter. She sniffed the air, then jumped down and moved to the teal velvet sofa.

"Is that a critique of my cooking?" Odette asked with a laugh. She tasted a bit of cream sauce on the wooden spoon, then added more salt. "I think it's delicious."

It was one of Odette's favorite meals. Her fiancé had loved it, too. The last time she'd made it had been for him. They had been celebrating his promotion. She had sat at the table listening to him talk about his career path and what this would mean for their future. She remembered thinking how much she didn't care and then thinking about how her life was turning into that Matchbox Twenty song, "Rest Stop." She had forced herself to think about how happy he was…how happy she was to have him. But they weren't happy, and it would only be just a little more than a month later when he would be the courageous one and admit it out loud.

Sadness filled Odette's chest. Or was it loneliness? She spooned the contents of the non-stick pan into a bowl, grabbed a fork, and went to sit next to the cat. She wanted to be done with grieving a relationship and a future that would have been less than either party deserved. She wanted to move forward and, for now, that meant eating alone while watching a competition cooking show.

Hepburn grumbled.

"I'm not alone. Sorry. I didn't mean to insult you." Odette giggled and then shoveled food into her mouth.

Hepburn purred then tucked her head under her paws.

Her show cut to a commercial, and a sad song played as the

soundtrack to a coming attraction. The notes bounced in Odette's head, forming a duet with the memory of the music from the abandoned theater.

*No, I'm not doing this.* Odette switched the channel and stabbed a chunk of zucchini with her fork. *I am not obsessing over this little mysterious lapse in my sanity and letting my imagination try to turn myths into reality. Nope!* She chewed with ferocious resolve as she returned to her regularly scheduled program.

# CHAPTER 5
# ODETTE

All night, Odette dreamed of a sorrowful concert played on a stage of red roses. She tossed and turned with every key change, waking in the wee hours tempted to call a psychiatrist. Her brain had been known to latch onto the tiniest thing and then twist around it until she felt like she would snap. This was only the latest screw coiling her anxiety. Chances are it would pass. One less cup of coffee and an extra dose of her herbal supplement, and it would most likely fade from her brain.

But the problem with anxiety is that *most likely* is not a good enough probability. She could bolster her odds by facing the source head-on...or getting as close as possible. To her topsy-turvy thoughts, that meant following through on the suggestion to ask the old woman who tended the roses. It didn't make sense. Another point of view on a silly ghost story wouldn't solve anything, would it? But anxiety isn't logical and so, to Odette, this became a very valid plan for her mental peace. She mulled it over all day. While shelving books, drinking tea, and between Isabelle's colorful anecdotes, Odette ruminated on this future conversation that would free her from the mild torment of this most superfluous problem.

"Hello?" Odette said, standing by the garden gate for the second time in twenty-four hours.

The sister turned, pruning shears in her hand. "You've returned! Come in, come in." She waved.

Odette opened the gate and took just two small steps into the courtyard. Her body hummed with the slight uptick in adrenaline.

"I'm Sister Mary Cecilia." She pulled off dirty gloves and reached out her crinkled fingers.

"It's nice to meet you, Sister." Odette shook her hand. "I'm Odette Durand."

"Ah, yes, Isabelle's new hire."

"You know Isabelle?" For a big city, it *was* beginning to feel more and more like a small town.

"She and I play cards together on Friday nights." Sister Mary Cecilia chuckled and walked back toward the roses. "She's been very excited to have your help."

"I think I will very much enjoy working for her." Odette looked around at the sweet garden. It was just nearing spring as young plants filled clay pots. Raised beds held sprouts standing in neat lines. Green leaves adorned two small trees. It was a tiny Eden in the middle of the city. But the centerpiece had to be the rose vines. They were lush and vibrant, budding too early in the year, like they were enchanted somehow. Or perhaps the nun just had a very green thumb.

"Oh, you will. She's got so many stories; you'll be entertained for years." Mary Cecilia chuckled again then turned her head just a bit, inclining her ear toward the theater as the same song began to play. Then she seemed to snap back to reality. "But you needed something? Here I am just going on about Isabelle and I completely halted your purpose in stopping in. Did you want to know more about the roses? They are almost supernatural, aren't they? Some of the Maker's finest handiwork, if I do say so myself."

Odette giggled. "The rosebuds are quite sweet, but no, what

caught my attention was the..." If she said it, there was no turning back, no unsaying it. If she was crazy there would be no ignoring it. But the sister had heard it too, hadn't she? She looked like she had. "The reason I stopped by again was..."

"Yes, dear?" Sister Mary Cecilia blinked her eyes at Odette.

"What caught my attention was the...well it was...uh...the music." Odette winced, waiting for some laughter or a call to the psych ward.

Sister Mary Cecilia didn't laugh or even look freaked out. She did widen her eyes as though the admission was a little surprising, but not nearly the reaction Odette imagined. "You hear the music?"

"Yes...don't you?" Odette leaned forward and raised her eyebrow.

The sister slapped her hip. "Of course I do. It's not imaginary."

"But you were surprised I heard it?"

"Most people don't stop and listen, so they miss a lot of the music around them, especially the sad songs. We don't want to be reminded of the sadness in this world."

Odette breathed in the woman's words. They were wise and deep, and a bit of a diversion...something still didn't add up. Odette crossed her arms over her chest. "Where, or should I say, who is it coming from? Isn't the theater abandoned? Is someone fixing it up? Would someone break into it just to play a dusty old piano?"

"Your sass is not lost on me, dear," Sister Mary Cecilia scolded, then smirked as she put her gardening gloves back on. "But the question you are really asking is, is the theater haunted?" She pointed her pruning shears at Odette then chuckled. "I take it someone has already wiled you with tales of phantoms?"

"So you're saying it isn't haunted? There's no phantom?"

"Do you really believe there could be?" Sister Mary Cecilia crossed her arms over her chest, mimicking Odette's pose.

"No one else hears the music," Odette replied. "If it's not something magical, then…"

"I never said it wasn't something magical, possibly miraculous…" the sister turned back to her roses, "or at least something miraculous in the making." She cut a rosebud from the vine and offered it to Odette. "I can assure you there is no ghost in that theater, dearie. Not much else I could offer would bring further surety."

Odette opened her mouth to ask another question, but the sly grin on the sister's face let her know there would be no more answers given. She looked at Odette as though she had divulged mountains of information and it should be enough. It wasn't even close. Her plan to thwart her anxiety had failed and her curiosity was taking over. Odette wanted to know so much more, but she remained silent and simply took the rose, careful not to prick her finger on the thorns. She lifted it to her nose and inhaled the sweet scent of its folded crimson petals. They were velvet against her fingers. "Thank you for this," Odette said.

"You're welcome." Sister Mary Cecilia went back to tending the flowers, filling her basket with more cut blooms.

Odette exited, closing the noisy gate behind her. She gave the sister a last look, another question waiting on the tip of her tongue.

"Don't ask questions you aren't ready to hear the answer to," Mary Cecilia said with barely a glance over her shoulder at Odette, who nodded and turned on her heel toward her apartment.

# CHAPTER 6
# BASTIAN

Bastian's fingers glided over the dusty piano keys. He could press them, feel the smooth surface beneath his calloused tips, yet he never left any prints or smudges. He was a walking illusion; there but not. A shimmer or shadow in the solid world. It was a torture that he should be used to, but there were still plenty of days when he wished he couldn't touch this world at all. He wanted to fade into oblivion. The music kept him sane...sad, but sane. So he played—his emotions and memories and longings becoming the melancholy melody that echoed off the dark, empty walls of the theater.

"Cheer up, dearie," the old nun's jovial voice reached Bastian's ears just after the clicking echo of her shoes on the hard floor.

"Shouldn't you have given up on me being cheery a while ago," he replied, pausing his fingers, leaving them hovering just over the piano keys.

"Nonsense," Sister Mary Cecilia scoffed as she passed him without a glance, not that she could offer one. She pulled the dead roses from the glass vase, which sat on the top of the piano, replacing them with fresh-cut buds.

"Why do you come here, Sister?" Bastian spun himself on the

piano bench so that his back was to her, not that she would know.

"I come here to bring you fresh flowers, to offer a smile, to let you know you aren't alone in this world." She came to sit down next to him.

He scooted a bit so she wouldn't sit on him. "But why? Why bother with the likes of me? Kindness doesn't break curses."

"Of course it does." The sister stared straight ahead. "It breaks the curse of loneliness, if even just for a moment."

"I am a lost cause."

She inclined her gaze in the direction of his voice. "You are particularly gloomy today and I think you have two options: tell me why or snap out of it."

Bastian laughed; a frustrated chuckle that burst from his throat. "Is being cursed for a hundred years not reason enough?"

"No, especially not when curses might be closer to being broken." One corner of the nun's mouth curled upward into a knowing grin.

Bastian stood to his feet and began pacing the floor in front of her. Her gaze shifted toward the floor, possibly hearing his feet pattering back and forth. He stopped right in front of her, but her eyes didn't leave the floor. "Do not be cruel, Sister."

"I would never." She put a hand on her chest. "There was a young woman. She stopped in the courtyard as I was cutting your roses...she heard the music."

The words hit him like a punch to his chest. "What does that matter? You hear the music. It means nothing." He started pacing again.

"We both know that isn't true. I hear the music because I care for you like a son, I know that you are real. A divine gift to keep you tethered to hope. If this girl, Odette, hears the music, then it must be for a reason." Sister Mary Cecilia patted the spot next to her on the piano bench.

Even though the old nun couldn't see him to tell, Bastian

obediently sat next to her again. "Odette?" Her name, sweet like a song. "Are you sure she hears it? Me?"

"She told me so herself," the sister replied. "Someone, probably Lizzie at the coffee shop, has her thinking it's all part of some old ghost story, which is ridiculous."

"Is it?" Bastian laughed again, but this time it was full of mirth.

"You aren't a ghost, dearie. You have to have died to be a ghost."

"Semantics."

"Truth."

Bastian felt dead. At least, he certainly didn't feel alive.

"I think this Odette is something special. It could mean something." Sister Mary Cecilia stood up slowly on stiff legs and picked up her flower basket.

"I can't get my hopes up," Bastian responded.

"Then don't," she smiled. "But be watchful for a new young woman, petite and pale. Blondish hair and…"

"…striking hazel eyes?"

"Yes, you've seen her already?"

Bastian swallowed. "Yes, the other morning while I was on the trolley. And I think…it couldn't have been…but if what you say is true…"

"Spit it out, dearie," Sister Mary Cecilia interrupted his pondering.

"She saw me."

The sister dropped her basket. It hit the floor and the dead flowers bounced, some over the edge and onto the chipped planks. "She saw you and she heard the music. This can't mean nothing, dear child."

"It doesn't mean that the curse will be broken." Bastian wanted to believe. He wanted to share the nun's optimism. There were too many variables, too many unknowns. There was no place for hope…not yet. But hope was edging in nonetheless, like a new harmony.

"Time will tell." She bent down to pick up her basket, then headed for the exit. "Time will tell, dearie," she sang over her shoulder.

Bastian began to smile, but the moment of peace and possibility was stolen away by a chilled breeze. It made the glass of the neglected chandeliers jingle and rattle above him, and blew the dust covers off some of the ratty seats. Then a shadow passed over, blocking the sunset light that gleamed through the grimy windows. It was large and looming, flying over like a bird of prey. Then it was gone. But Bastian still felt cold.

# CHAPTER 7

# ODETTE

hapter Three Books stayed quite busy all morning. It kept Odette on her toes, bustling about the shop helping customers find their perfect weekend read while Isabelle hosted the monthly seniors' book club. The club's laughter echoed through the stacks, loud little outbursts of joy interrupting the otherwise quiet atmosphere. It was nice, the laughter and the helping patrons. Odette enjoyed matching people with the perfect book. She always believed that everyone loved reading, and that those who didn't think so just hadn't found the right book yet.

In between customers, she looked for a book of her own. But she wasn't hunting for a cozy romance or a mysterious thriller. She searched for ghost stories, one in particular. There had to be more than just word-of-mouth accounts of the theater ghost. The way Lizzie talked, it had been a pretty popular legend in the Quarter, and that meant there must be more information. Didn't it? Or was she still just a little too obsessed with nonsense? She entertained the idea that she was going crazy, or being pranked by the locals, and needed to forget the whole thing and find something better to do with her free time. She couldn't. She'd heard the music. It was real. The sister could hear it too. If it wasn't a musically skillful squatter, what was it? That little old lady had Odette feeling like there was way more to the story than Lizzie, or maybe anyone, knew.

"Teatime," Isabelle called from the corner by the chairs.

Odette abandoned her search and sank into one of the worn, high-back seats while Isabelle poured the steaming tea.

"Everything okay?" Isabelle dropped two cubes of sugar into each teacup and they plopped with a little splash that almost escaped over the rims.

"Oh, it's fine," Odette picked up her delicate cup and stirred it before taking a sip. "I was looking for a book and just can't seem to find what I need."

"Well, honey, you have come to the right woman!" Isabelle exclaimed. "I know every book on these shelves, so tell me what it is you're looking for."

"A ghost story—a specific one." Odette took another sip of the black tea. "A local legend."

"You might have to be more specific. New Orleans has more than one ghost story to tell." Isabelle dunked a shortbread cookie into her tea.

"Well..." Odette paused. She felt silly now. It was just a story and there were several explanations for the music. She didn't believe in ghosts. But she told herself that same thing for two days and couldn't get past it. Maybe reading the story would help her find some closure and return her dwindling sanity. "Well, I was wondering about the theater ghost. Lizzie said legend has it you can still hear him playing piano...if you listen or something...it sounded interesting."

"There's a lot of tales but that might be one of my favorites. It's obscure though, not much telling about it outside of the Quarter." Isabelle tapped a finger on the side of her teacup.

"So no books about it?"

"Didn't say that." Isabelle set her cup down and stood up. "I think it shows up in one or two anthologies." She walked directly to a bookshelf in the far corner of the shop, bent down to see the third shelf from the bottom, and drew her finger across each spine until she found what she was looking for. "Here." She pulled two books from that shelf and then a third from the shelf above. "These should have what you are looking for."

Odette took the books and read each title. They were all collections of New Orleans ghost stories and legends. "Thank you."

"You're welcome." Isabelle retrieved her tea and took a sip. "That top one was written by a local author and researcher, so it'd be where I start. Or finish, depending on how you want to approach the topic."

"Sounds good. I'll ring myself up before I leave."

"Nonsense! Just borrow them and bring them back when you're finished. Perks of working in a bookshop." Isabelle winked.

Odette smiled and picked up a cookie from the little tray to nibble.

"Can I ask why you're so interested in this particular ghost story? Besides Lizzie's mention?" Isabelle poured herself another cup of tea.

Odette stared down into her cup like the brown liquid would offer a response that didn't make her sound looney.

"You heard the music?" Isabelle grinned over the rim of her cup. Her eyes were wide and shining.

"I heard music from the theater," Odette replied, "not necessarily *the* music." She took a bigger bite of the cookie and with her mouth full added, "The nun, what's her name, she just had me thinking."

"Ah, you've met Sister Mary Cecilia," Isabelle chuckled. "She owes me five dollars from our last card game." The shop owner finished her last sip of tea. "She hears the music too, ya know."

Odette swallowed the rest of the cookie. "She said as much."

"And knowing her, she didn't say much else."

"Not really, but she made me feel like there was more to this story."

"She has a way of doing that, but don't let her get in your head. There have been dozens of people who've sworn they heard the music over the years, most eventually concluded that it was just a vagabond or transient sleeping in the theater who could play piano, no ghost. And I'm as eccentric as they come so if I don't think there's a ghost..."

"I don't even believe in ghosts." Odette swigged the last of her now lukewarm tea. "But the story has me intrigued."

"It's a simple one compared to some other doozies out there, but there is something about it that draws the curiosity out of a person. Mostly, I think it's because in a hundred years no one has bought that theater to renovate it or tear it down or turn it into some nightclub or apartment complex. Adds an air of the theatrical to an otherwise lackluster tale." Isabelle collected the remnants of their afternoon tea back onto the tray. "Either way I hope you enjoy the reading."

Odette watched Isabelle exit to the little kitchenette in the back room. Then she picked the top book from off the stack and flipped to the table of contents, intending to read a bit while things were quiet. The doorbell dinged, signaling the arrival of a new customer and the postponement of that plan.

It was dark outside when Odette exchanged ballet flats for fuzzy socks as she curled up on her sofa to finally read about the theater ghost. A bowl of popcorn and a dark chocolate bar were on the side table along with a tall glass of cherry coke.

"Girl dinner," Odette said to Hepburn before shoving a handful of popcorn into her mouth.

The black cat sniffed at the bowl of buttered kernels then jumped onto the couch and strolled across Odette's lap before curling up into a purring ball on her chest.

"Make yourself comfortable," Odette whispered to the little cat, giggling to herself as the cat merely purred louder and closed its eyes to doze off.

Odette pulled a fluffy, fleece blanket over her legs and grabbed the first book, finding just the story she was interested in. She read over it twice because it was so short. She repeated the process with the second book in between mouthfuls of popcorn, ignoring Hepburn's grumblings when kernels would fall onto her fur. The third was the one Isabelle said was written by a local, so she had saved it for last, hoping it would be best.

*In the nineteen twenties, The Castle Rose theater was a hot spot in New Orleans: dinner, booze, and plenty of music. Most nights, the star attraction was a young pianist, Bastian Roux. By seventeen, he had saved enough money for passage on one of the big steamships and immigrated to America, making his home in the Big Easy. He was known to say it didn't matter that his mother was French and his father British because he was one hundred percent New Orleans and one hundred percent in love with this city. Friends and theater patrons knew him as being full of life and joy, and a gifted musician. The way he mastered the keys could make anyone get up and dance, then just as easily and quickly bring the whole crowd to tears.*

"At least they didn't say, 'He could light up a room,'" Odette chuckled to herself. It was so cliché to have people talk about victims like they were saints. Just once, she'd like a true crime story where someone was a little more honest. Let them say, "They were full of life and joy on good days, but man, they lost their salvation when stuck in rush-hour traffic." She took a bite of her chocolate bar and continued reading.

*At the height of his local fame, Bastian suddenly disappeared. With no word or warning, he seems to have just vanished.*

"Dun. Dun. Dun!" Odette sang. Hepburn lifted her head to grumble at the interruption to her nap.

*It was alarming to his fans and employers, who swore foul play was involved. Rumors spread about what might have happened. The most popular being that Bastian was murdered by a rival after a heated argument and then buried under the bowels of the theater. The police did, in fact, run an investigation at the time, but never found any evidence of what had happened to the young, up-and-coming star.*

"One, I am not going looking for corpses in old basements. Two, how could there be no evidence at all if there was a murder? No leads? No suspects? No transcripts of interrogations?" Odette was sure there were one or two podcasters or TikTokers out there who would have had this solved by now if given old crime scene photos and a set of public records.

*In a town full of voodoo, whispers of a curse started circling and claimed the life of the theater. With no other musicians willing to take the stage, and fewer and fewer customers willing to risk whatever evil they thought stole Bastian away in the night, The Castle Rose theater closed.*

*A curse.* That was the stuff of fairytales. But superstition could be a powerful thing. "Was some sort of mass hysteria happening? If we all think there's a ghost playing sad jazz, do we hear the sad jazz?" Odette asked Hepburn, who ignored her completely. For a split second, Odette thought she had unlocked the key to everything. Then she remembered that she had heard the music before she had ever heard the story, so she probably wasn't being infected by some totem. She felt a touch of relief at that realization.

*After a while, the public seemed to forget about Bastian and the theater, until one fall night, after midnight, a young woman, Charlotte Andrews, was walking home down the foggy streets. Ms. Andrews says as she passed the theater, she could hear music playing—piano music— but there were no lights and no person to be found hiding in the abandoned building. Police found no evidence of a recent intruder. The rumor mill started back up and resurrected the story of Bastian Roux, the musician, some now believed to be cursed to spend his afterlife haunting the dreary remains of The Castle Rose and filling the back streets of the French Quarter with his spooky lullaby.*

"Oh please," Odette rolled her eyes at the cheesy writing. She closed the book and tossed it back onto the table with the others.

Hepburn elicited an annoyed growl as Odette sat up, causing the cat to lose its comfortable position.

"Sorry, my little dragon cat," Odette responded to the feline. She grabbed her laptop from the coffee table.

The books had offered little more than Lizzie had in the cafe the other morning; all conjecture about a musician who disappeared with no explanation. Whether they spun it into a tale of murder, vamped about voodoo curses, or romanticized it into a tragic love story…it was all just myth. Except for the musician. The last book gave him a name, and with a name, Odette could use her superpower – Google.

She typed away on her little keyboard, hit enter, and left the computer on the table while she padded to the kitchen to refill her soda. The rose that Sister Mary Cecilia gifted her sat in a glass on her counter. She had added a little sugar and apple cider vinegar to the water, a secret her grandmother taught her to keep the gorgeous flower alive a little longer. It had begun to bloom, with large petals opening themselves up to the world. Odette smelled its fragrance even from a couple of feet away. She inhaled deeply and then returned to her spot on the couch.

She gulped the ice-cold soda before setting her cup down and turning her attention back to her computer screen. Scrolling past the first couple of results, which were all just links to the book she had just been reading, she came across a photo. Odette covered her mouth with her hand. Staring back at her, in fuzzy black and white, was a face she recognized.

"It couldn't be," she whispered to herself as she pulled the device closer to her. She pushed her glasses up on her nose and squinted at the image.

A young man sat beside a piano. He was dressed in black pants and a light gray shirt with suspenders and a tie that hung loose around his neck. He had curly hair that was a haphazard mop on top of his head and thin features. He was smiling, a big smile, one that took up his entire face and made his eyes bright, even in a photograph. The eyes are what threw her, the joy that exuded from them. This couldn't be the same man she'd seen on the trolley her first morning in the Quarter. Besides the fact that this picture was taken a hundred years ago, this man was happy, and the one she'd observed through glass had looked…oh so lost and lonely.

Odette stood up and paced back and forth in front of the coffee table, stopping every few rounds to give the image another look.

"No, this is definitely my imagination getting the best of me," she muttered to herself.

Hepburn jumped up on the coffee table and rubbed her face and neck against the computer. She meowed.

"Exactly," Odette responded. "I have let this all get to me. I've let it mess with my head and it has brought on some hallucination. That's it. Besides, I only saw trolley-guy for like thirty seconds from several yards away so this could just be a trick of the mind. Similar hair and my memory has gotten all jumbled with my crazy and so I think it's the same guy from this photo, but it's not." Odette sat back down on the sofa and sighed. "It's not, right?" She asked Hepburn who meowed then pranced off toward the kitchen.

"You're very reassuring," Odette called after her furry companion. She stared at the photo one last time. The image bore an uncanny resemblance to the man on the trolley, it made her soul jump like an acrobat in her chest. "It's just the caffeine and the crazy talking. Mom always said I knew how to run away with a thing and make it more dramatic than it needed to be." She shut the laptop and plopped herself against the back of the couch. "That's what's happening now. This is not a ghost story come to life. I don't believe in ghosts." She didn't. But her thoughts continued to spiral around the topic. Either she was becoming a little more open-minded to the idea, or she was losing her mind completely. It was probably the latter.

# CHAPTER 8
# BASTIAN

Bastian stood next to a lamppost and watched the drizzle fall around him. Gray clouds, which matched his mood, hid the afternoon sun. From around the street corner, he heard a brass band play a funeral dirge. A slow jazz beat underscored the melody of an old hymn. It got louder until the band came into view, turning onto Bastian's street, all dressed in black suits. A parade master, wearing a hat and sash, and decked out in all the proper regalia of his position, led the assembly one soulful step at a time, in rhythm to the music.

Just behind them came two dark horses pulling a wagon on which laid a black casket adorned with white flowers. On either side and behind were family and friends making up the first line. They were dressed to the nines and holding a variety of colorful parasols and handkerchiefs—a bright contrast to the otherwise gloomy scene—that they slowly and methodically twirled and waved above their heads. Some of them cried. Others sang along to the band's rendition of "Just a Closer Walk with Thee."

Bastian found the lyrics drifting into his mind and exiting in a quiet hum. *When my feeble life is o'er, Time for me will be no more; Guide me gently, safely o'er; To Thy kingdom shore, to Thy shore.* He almost laughed at the irony. Then he almost wept for the longing. Once upon a time, he thought death was the enemy, but now he would welcome it like a long-lost friend. He would relish being laid in the casket and led down the street in a procession of music.

Bastian stepped off the curb and joined the other neighbors and tourists in the second line. He didn't shuffle or dance, he just marched, one step at a time behind the mourners who wailed and sang. The sky darkened. A flash of shadow cast over him and he realized it wasn't a brewing storm but the tortuous companion who haunted him. It flew by like a cold wind until it found a home hovering over the casket. Bastian watched the horses twitch and snort under its presence. A shiver ran down his spine and arms to the tips of his fingers. He shoved his hands in his pockets and kept walking, not knowing why he didn't just retreat.

About three blocks further down the street there was a shift in the music. The rhythm of the hymns began to pick up their pace, an announcement that it was nearly time to "cut the body loose". Turning another corner the trumpeter began a new tune. Wailing turned to laughter as the first and second liners began to dance more fully, writhing and moving in celebration. As if on cue, sunlight poked holes in the cloud cover and the shadow over the casket dissolved into light. Bastian took his leave of the festivities, returning to the part of a spectator on the sidewalk.

Cheers, shouting, and singing of a new song filled the streets. Long ago, Bastian would have reveled until the very last note. Unseen and unknown as he was, he still felt as though his melancholy demeanor would diminish the experience somehow. He was a misfit among the lively passersby and bystanders. So he watched from a distance. He watched the tourists take photos and videos—he could never understand this new obsession with documenting every moment on pocket devices. He watched the shop owners clap along from their doorways. He watched the neighbors peer from their balconies and windows. He watched each face until one stopped his watching.

It was her. The girl with the in-between eyes and in-between hair—now pulled back into a ponytail and off her face. She stood on one of the iron balconies, leaning against the railing and sipping from a yellow coffee mug while she watched the funeral. Her coral lips stretched into a wondrous smile. Bastian couldn't take his eyes off her. He tried. He wanted to. But he couldn't. Something about her pulled him in and held him. Perhaps he was hung up on the notion that she had looked at him the other morning. That she'd truly seen him from her spot near the trolley stop and that her smile had really been for him. That she could be the same girl Sister Mary Cecilia had spoken with, the girl who had heard him play.

"Impossible." He shook his head and looked down at his feet. It was nonsense. Wanting it to be anything else was utter foolishness. He had been hopeful before, and it had come to nothing. It always came to nothing.

Bastian took two steps in the direction of the theater before stopping and allowing himself one last look in her direction. If she had been staring at the procession, or even gone, it would have been a grace, a reminder of his place. But she was neither of those things. The in-between girl stared at him, the in-between boy, looking directly at his face. Her eyes darted back and forth, her mouth hung slightly open. She grabbed the black rail and leaned forward like she was trying to get a closer look.

"You!" she called out to him.

No. She wasn't talking to him. She was looking through him. But when he looked around, there was no one else, it was only him.

"Wait there!" she yelled again before turning to run into her apartment.

Bastian's heart thumped harder and faster, and his lungs fought for breath. If she saw him, he should wait. He should be sure. But what if she didn't? Could he stand the disappointment? Waiting was inconceivable because *he* was inconceivable. Hope was inconceivable. What did it matter if she saw him or not? The sister talked of breaking curses but curses like his were not meant to be broken because *he* was too broken.

Bastian didn't wait. He hurried into the crowd, almost running back to the security of his theater. Behind him, he heard her.

"Bastian?"

Did she say his name? No, he'd misheard. He had to have misheard. He didn't turn around. He only walked faster until he was sure the possibility of her reaching him was gone. He pulled his coat tighter around him and popped the collar up around his neck. He took deep breaths trying to regulate his body and mind. Something wet dripped down his cheek. He told himself it was the rain, even though he knew he couldn't feel the rain.

## CHAPTER 9
# OCTAVIAN

Octavian Zane sipped a steaming espresso from a tiny white cup while sitting at a cafe table outside a quaint little bistro in Rome. It was his third trip to Europe this year, consulting with museums and galleries. He dealt in classic art and antiquities, though he cared very little for the past. He merely found a profession that afforded him the things he did love: money, luxury, and travel to beautiful places. And it was easy. Being alive for a century offered one a certain advantage in this line of work. A few commissions could establish his financial stability for a year and allow him several months to relish life, indulging in all its delights.

Today, the sun felt warm, and his espresso tasted strong. He tipped back the last swallow and set the cup down on the table, the porcelain clanking against the iron. He took the cloth napkin and wiped the corner of his mouth before tossing it next to the cup. Then he stood, adjusting his black tie and his black vest before pulling his matching suit jacket from where he had carefully laid it on the back of a chair. He draped it over his arm as he prepared to stroll back down the lane to the antique shop with which he was doing business. As he stepped onto the cobblestone street, he pulled his pocket watch from his vest and ran his thumb over the ornate gold exterior. He traced the outline of the coiled snake engraved on the case. He flipped it open with his thumb to check the time. It was a habit more than anything else because this watch hadn't told the time in a hundred years. Forever stopped at 1:58.

He smiled at the reminder of his power and immortality. About to flip it closed again, he stopped. His grin straightened and his breath quickened to match the increasing rhythm of his thumping heart. With a singular, faint tick the second hand moved. He thought it was only his imagination, but it moved again and again and again. Tick. Tick. Tick. The whisper of it grew louder and louder in his eardrums until it was booming inside his brain—the noise of it competing with the noise of his pulse. He stared at the watch face, the thin hand making its journey full circle until it came back to twelve and the minute hand joined the excursion.

"No," Octavian growled to himself. He slammed the watch closed and returned it to his pocket.

Changing course, Octavian crossed the street and shuffled through the milling passersby as he headed back to his hotel. He ignored the doorman's greeting and didn't even glance at the elevator. He took the stairs two at a time until he reached his suite on the twelfth floor. He fumbled with the key, but as soon as the door unlocked he rushed inside, securing it anew. He dropped his jacket on the bed and went straight to the bathroom.

Standing over the marble sink, he turned on the faucet to splash some cold water on his pallid face in hopes the frigid liquid would bring him back to his senses. Wake him up from this walking dream. After all, this had to be a fluke. A momentary lapse in his sanity and nothing more.

Octavian blinked his gray-blue eyes, then pulled out the pocket watch again. "It was nothing. I didn't see what I thought I saw. I didn't hear it. It was the sun playing tricks on my eyes." He kept muttering to himself. His hands trembled just a little as he flipped the watch open. 2:13. "This. Isn't. Happening." He snarled through clenched teeth and smashed his palms repeatedly against the counter until his skin stung.

Octavian paused, hands on the sink, weight leaning on his arms. He looked down at the floor and took three deep breaths. "Pull yourself together. You are not some child whose toy has been taken away. You will not lose yourself." He straightened his tie and tugged his vest. Then he ran both hands through his now disheveled hair, smoothing himself back into place.

Catching his reflection in the mirror, Octavian was caught off guard by something. There was a spot of light mingled amongst his dark locks. He leaned forward to get a closer look. On the right side of his head, a thin strand of hair was fading from black to gray, like the ebony color was being chased from his roots right out of the tips. His chest tightened and a cold feeling flowed down his veins and out his fingertips in a similar fashion.

There was definitely some magic at work. "What are you up to, Bastian Roux?"

Octavian hadn't uttered that name in several decades. He thought it every day, but never spoke it out loud, had never had the need to. He loathed the taste of it now, almost as much as the idea of going back to a place he would rather be rid of. But there was no getting around it. Some things one must deal with in person.

He returned to his room and began to pack his belongings into his brown leather duffel bag. He picked up his phone and dialed his assistant. "I need you to let my client know there was an emergency, and that I will have to postpone our dealings. I'll also need you to book me a flight…to New Orleans."

# CHAPTER 10
# ODETTE

After realizing she was outside, on the sidewalk, in sweats and fuzzy socks, Odette returned to her apartment reeling at the idea that the man on the street had been trolley-guy. More importantly, trolley-guy looked even more like Bastian Roux—a dead jazz musician—than she'd first thought upon seeing his pixelated image two days ago. And said dead musician had looked right at her. He had seen her, and she had seen him, and she was not insane. She sounded insane. She could see where someone else might think she was insane. But Odette was certain she was not crazy…mostly certain.

She changed into some jeans and a black t-shirt, then pulled on a pair of slip-on sneakers, almost falling over in the process. Walking through the kitchen, she gulped the now cold coffee in her mug and gave Hepburn a quick scratch behind the ears before grabbing her jacket, purse, and keys. "I'll be back later," she whispered to her cat as she closed and locked her apartment door.

She marched the four blocks toward the theater without distraction. Well, she did pause for a second when the aroma of coffee wafted over her senses, tempted to stop into Madame Clary's for a latte, but decided that could wait and continued down the street. She had a mystery to solve. If the music was real and Bastian was real, then maybe he would be there, and she would see him again and talk to him and prove she wasn't crazy once and for all...ghost or no ghost. If he wasn't, then... well...she'd figure that out later.

Now she needed to figure out how one would get into an old theater that had been condemned and its doors boarded shut. So she walked around the perimeter, trying to find an entrance that didn't take a crowbar to open. She rubbed the side of her hand across the dingy windows, smudging the layer of grime enough to peer inside like she was hoping someone would take pity on her and let her in, but that was a little ridiculous, because who would let her in? The dead musician? Could he even open doors? Was she believing in ghosts now?

"There's a door around the back, a service entrance."

Odette rounded on her heel, startled by the sweet voice. It was the sister she'd met a few days before. "I...uh...I was just..."

"You were trying to get into the theater. I assume to see Bastian." The woman smiled.

Odette opened her mouth, but no words came out. *He's real.*

The woman held out her hand. "I'm Sister Mary Cecilia. We met a few days ago."

Odette shook her warm hand. "I remember. You gave me the rose."

Sister Mary Cecilia's smile doubled in size, and her eyes brightened. "I was wondering when you'd be back."

"Because I heard the music?"

"And because you strike me as the type of person who doesn't let things like this go," the sister chuckled.

"I don't," Odette replied. "Why didn't you just tell me about Bastian Roux, since you obviously know more of the story than you let on?"

"Don't tap your little foot at me, dearie." Sister Mary Cecilia put her hands on her round hips. "First of all, do you know how many people come around here asking about the legend and

Bastian and if they can see the theater? And do you know how many of them are just looking to write a story or make some sort of video that is supposed to go viral, or some such thing and they don't care one bit about anything other than their own spotlight?"

"I don't care about Instagram followers or YouTube views," Odette mumbled, averting her gaze to her shoes like a child being reprimanded.

"No, I don't suppose you do. But even then, the story wasn't mine to tell."

Odette looked back at Sister Mary Cecilia. "So you've seen him too?"

"No, but I take it you have and that is curious indeed. Over the years, there have been a few who have heard the music, but none have actually seen him, myself included."

"Well, I think I saw him." Odette doubted herself. It was a glance from a distance and a fuzzy old picture. Perhaps it wasn't him after all. There was still time to find she was only crazy.

"Don't go second-guessing yourself now. Bastian doesn't need any of that negativity. He makes enough of it all on his own."

"How did you…?"

The sister patted Odette's arm. "I'm good at reading the parts of people they don't think anyone else sees. I pay attention."

"I came here to see him up close. To know for sure."

"Then go see him."

"What do I say?" Odette asked. What does one say to a ghost?

"I'd start with *hello*," the sister said with another quiet laugh. "I'll show you to the door."

Odette nodded and followed Sister Mary Cecilia into the courtyard and past the rosebushes to a narrow doorway that was almost hidden by the vines of English ivy trying to mingle with the red blooms. The sister pulled out an old brass skeleton key from her pocket and turned it in the door's lock. There was a click, then she pulled the creaking door open.

"Go ahead." The sister gestured for Odette to step inside.

"Are you coming with me?"

"No, but I'll be right out here if you need me," Sister Mary Cecilia said.

Odette nodded once more and took a deep breath before stepping forward with clenched fists.

She squinted, letting her eyes adjust to the darkness of the corridor. The dusty air tickled her nose and something tickled the back of her neck. Odette jumped and swatted, thinking it was a spider, but it was just a long cobweb hanging from the rafters. A layer of dust covered everything and draped like gossamer curtains from ceiling lights and the paintings that hung on the walls.

It got darker the further into the theater Odette walked, so she pulled out her phone and turned on the flashlight feature. About thirty feet inside, the corridor split into two. To the right was what looked to have been a kitchen. Her small beam of light glared off metal shelves that had been knocked onto the ground. Pipes and wires protruded from the walls where she assumed appliances used to reside. There were broken dishes and papers and old silver utensils strewn over the floor.

Pulling back and going to the right, the hallway opened into a large room with a high ceiling. Tables and chairs filled the space. Some were covered with white sheets, while others were knocked over or broken. Through the chaos and dilapidation, you could still sense what once was. Tall windows and opulent chandeliers highlighted the luxury this place had once offered. Odette imagined it full of lively patrons in suits and silk dresses. Scanning over the room and dreaming of what it must have been like, she saw the stage. It was framed by antique bulbs, some now splintered and shattered. A dusty grand piano sat to one side, on top of which was a vase with fresh, bright red roses. She tiptoed toward them. Their sweet fragrance mingled with the musty air. She sneezed. The floor creaked somewhere behind torn velvet curtains.

Odette spun around, looking for the cause of the creaking.

"Who's there?" She pointed her light to the wings of the stage and silently chastised herself for being a scaredy-cat when she was the one to come looking for a ghost. "I know you're here."

More creaking came from the other side of the stage.

She changed direction and her flashlight caught the edge of a form before it hid itself again. "I saw you. I saw you on the trolley. I saw you on the street today. I heard the music, and I talked to the nun, so I know you're here and I know you're real, so just come on out ghost-boy." She walked forward with tentative steps, nudging herself closer to where the shadow had passed.

"Leave me alone." The voice, which held a bit of a mingled European accent, floated around her like it was without a form to anchor it to one spot. It wasn't angry or booming. It sounded sad.

"Sorry, I can't do that," Odette replied. "See, I have been feeling like I'm going crazy and I need to know I'm not, so…"

The piano banged out a D-minor. "Then look!"

Odette turned around again, feeling a bit dizzy. Standing behind the piano was Bastian Roux. He was taller than she'd expected and thin. His hair was a pile of disheveled curls, and his skin was pale, making his rosy lips and blue eyes stand out in contrast.

"There, do you feel better?" He scrunched his nose and his nostrils flared. He trembled.

"I…I…" Odette wasn't sure what exactly kept the words from escaping beyond her current stutter. Was it the angry glint in his eyes or the fact that, not only could she see Bastian, but she could also see through him? His transparent form only filtering the view of the room behind him. A chill ran down her arms.

"Spit it out, love." Bastian stepped from behind the piano and took two steps in her direction.

Odette took two steps backward. "I'm sorry."

"Sorry?"

"I didn't mean to…"

"No, you just didn't care. You didn't consider my feelings."

His quiet voice got louder, and he took another step closer. "Like everyone else, you thought only of yourself!" He reached and grabbed the vase and threw it down, shattering the crystal and making a mess of water and flowers on the wooden floor.

Odette jumped and dropped her phone. The light clicked off, and it was so dark she couldn't see Bastian.

"Go." A whisper blew cold against her cheek.

Odette fumbled to pick up her phone. When she had it back in hand and the space was once again illuminated, he was gone. She heard a creak and saw the curtains move. Now she was the one shaking, tremors moving in waves that began in the shudder of her shoulders and ended at her wobbly knees. She backed off the stage. The piano keys banged out another low note. She picked up her pace, running in the direction from which she had come. A scream that was more of an agonizing roar bounced off the walls around her and made her shiver. Odette didn't look back and didn't stop until she was outside.

"Oh, dear, I take it the introduction did not go well." Sister Mary Cecilia waited by the door as she had promised. Her wrinkled face drooped with concern. "What did you do?"

"Me? What did I do? What about him, the snarling beast who scared the living daylights out of me?" Odette rested her hands on her knees and took deep breaths to fill her aching lungs.

The sister gently pushed Odette to the side so she could close and lock the door. "Bastian can be temperamental, but he is no beast. I assure you, and if he is, then he is all bark and no bite."

"Well, the bark was enough."

"He can be frightful when he is scared." Sister Mary Cecilia looked at Odette. "I am sure the next time will go better."

"Next time? Oh, that won't be happening. I saw him. I'm not crazy, but I'm also not stupid and I'm not going to ruffle ghost-boy's feathers a second time and have him break something other than a vase. Something like me!"

"He broke my vase?" The sister's eyes widened, then squinted into a scowl. "I will most definitely have something to say to him about that. You can't just go breaking things that don't belong to you." She started to walk back into the abbey.

"And what about having a talk with him about not breaking me?" Odette huffed.

Sister Mary Cecilia turned around abruptly. "Well, you said you weren't going to go back, so I doubt that will be a concern." She looked Odette up and down. "Perhaps you aren't who I thought you were."

"What does that mean?"

"It means I thought you were someone who didn't let things go so easily, but I guess I was wrong." She returned to her exit without another word.

Odette stared, just blinking, for a while after the sister had gone inside and out of view. Little old lady or not, how dare she judge Odette's intentions? And who in their right mind would go back to talk to a ghost when he wanted no such thing? She wanted to see him, and she had. She wanted to be sure she wasn't crazy, and good news–she wasn't. But she was most certainly not going to spend another moment in the presence of Bastian Roux; scared, angry, beast or not. He was no longer her concern.

# CHAPTER II

# BASTIAN

Bastian watched her run away from behind the stage's crimson curtains. He had become so good at not being seen that it terrified him to have someone stare straight into his face. The sister was different. He didn't have to look her in the eye, only listen to her chastisements. But this woman, the presumed Odette, had looked into his eyes and he hadn't liked what she'd seen. Not that any of it mattered. She wouldn't be back. He would stay cursed.

"AHHH!" His pain roared out of his mouth—the ache of a caged animal crying out for freedom. He pulled at the curtains, and they ripped further to shreds.

Bastian ran his hand through his hair then did what he always did to calm his soul, he sat down at the piano. His fingers rested over the ivory. He inhaled, then exhaled, the music pushing out of him like breath. This was a sad song. That was all he played now. He only vaguely remembered when he used to play happy songs.

# INTERLUDE: BASTIAN, 1923

The lights made Bastian sweat, little beads dripping down his forehead and making his hair stick to his skin. He didn't care as he tapped his foot to the jazz tune and laughed as he played. The club patrons danced and snapped from their seats. Bastian felt larger than life on that stage. Endless. Boundless. Immortal. He slid his fingers over the keys, then hit the last two notes and was answered by an ovation that vibrated into his very heart. He stood and took a bow before jogging backstage.

"Great show tonight, Bas!" Jimmy, one of the stagehands, patted him on the back as he walked by.

"Thanks." Bastian grabbed a towel and rubbed it along the back of his neck and face. He reached for a glass of water and took a drink. It went down wrong, and he began to cough. He held the towel up to his mouth as he continued to grasp for a clean breath. When he was finally able to fill his lungs, he looked down and saw that the white fabric in his hands was stained red —a splatter of blood to remind him of his humanity.

Bastian rushed past the other musicians and stagehands and out the backstage door into the alley. The night air was cool and fresh against his warm skin and inside his burning chest.

"Beautiful night." Someone stepped out of the shadows toward Bastian.

"That it is." He folded the towel over to hide the evidence of his illness. "What do you want? I thought I already told you I wasn't interested in your schemes."

"I'm hurt at the insinuation, Bas. I only want to help my friend."

"Friends? Now you concede we're friends, Zane?" Bastian had known Octavian Zane since he first stepped off the ship and into New Orleans. He had tried to befriend the fellow creative soul, but Zane made it hard, keeping everyone just a bit at arm's length, until recently.

"We could be. I could help you," Octavian said.

Bastian laughed. "You heal the sick now?"

"I wouldn't say that." Octavian came to stand next to Bastian and leaned against the brick wall of the theater. "But you know as well as I that there is a lot about this city most don't see; strange and wondrous things…"

"Voodoo." Or was it hoodoo? Not that the difference mattered much to Bastian. He didn't even like saying the words. He'd heard whispers of magic but kept his distance from that sort of thing. It felt dark and dangerous.

"It can save you." Octavian tugged at the thin chain under his jacket to reveal a gold pocket watch embossed with a slithering serpent. "At the very least, it can offer you a little more time."

"Why do you care about how much time I have left?" Bastian chuckled again, and it caused him to cough again, making his mouth taste of copper. He wiped a dribble of blood from his bottom lip.

"Can't I just want to help you?" Octavian shrugged. His brow wrinkled and his lip curved in what might be concern.

"I'd like to believe that, but I think we both know you don't just want to help me. What's in it for you? What will this cure, or miracle, or whatever you want to call it, cost me?" Octavian always had a bottom line that was for his benefit. This wasn't about getting him the best table in the theater in exchange for free drinks. This was bigger, and the price would be too.

"You make it all sound so cold, friend." Octavian stood up straight and reached out, squeezing Bastian's shoulder. "What does the cost matter in exchange for your life? Besides, I don't want anything from you that you wouldn't be better off without."

Bastian pulled his shoulder from Octavian's grip. "I bet the devil says the same thing."

Octavian straightened his tie and jacket. He smirked. "Don't pretend like you and the devil aren't on speaking terms. You are no saint, Bastian Roux."

"No, I'm not," he sighed. He imagined saints weren't afraid of dying. He figured them to be heroes who stormed into death like it was merely the gateway to a new adventure. He shuddered at the thought of dying, and more so, of what came after. "And I'm not ready to die."

"Then give yourself more time to make peace with death." Octavian sidled up to Bastian, placing a hand back on his shoulder. "Who knows? Perhaps you can beat death altogether."

Bastian hesitated and then turned to face Zane. "How?" He couldn't believe he was even considering this proposal. He *wanted* to trust Octavian. He wanted to believe they were the friends—brothers—he had hoped they could and would be. But a little itch of a notion told him he shouldn't trust this. Even now, his stomach twisted in knots, seemingly begging him to wretch out the very thought of giving in to this madness. But he didn't have much time left. He could feel his body getting weaker, and his breathing was getting harder.

"Don't worry about the details. All you have to do is say yes, and I'll take care of everything else."

"I know it will cost me more than a 'yes,'" Bastian replied.

Octavian smiled and nodded slowly. "You can live, for years, maybe decades, centuries even. You can stay in the spotlight with all eyes and ears locked on you, cheering your name. You can travel. You can live a life most would only dream of and all without an ending. All you have to do is break your engagement with Catherine."

"What?"

"Tell Catherine you no longer wish to marry her." Octavian smoothed a hand over his dark hair.

"But I love her."

"Of course," Octavian said. "But as things are, you'll be dead in a couple of months and she'll be left alone, grieving you. So, either way, Catherine ends up heartbroken. My way, you don't die."

"But why?" Bastian coughed again.

Octavian smirked. "Let's just say that sometimes there has to be a breaking before a mending can take place. Or perhaps it's more of an exchange—a temporal sacrifice for something more eternal."

A growl rumbled in Bastian's throat. He spun on his heel and punched the brick wall. Pain stung his knuckles and rattled down his fingers. He shook his hand and started to cough again. He couldn't stop the hacking and his chest stung with every attempt at breathing. He bent over and could see the blood dripping from his mouth, felt it warm and wet on his lips and chin. He smelled the metallic bite as he looked up at Octavian, still wheezing. "Yes."

# CHAPTER 12

# BASTIAN, 2024

Bastian pounded his fists on the piano keys. He stood up, tossed the bench onto its side, and roared again until the pain turned to hot tears on his cold cheeks. He had been weak and selfish. He had watched the woman he loved weep and stutter and beg him to reconsider. She had gripped his hand, trying to keep him from walking out her door and he had forced her to let go and turned his back on her. The memory of her soft skin holding so tightly gripped his wrist even now. He rubbed it away, pulling at his skin until it felt like it would rip from his bones. He fell to his knees, his head hung over.

Cold air tickled his neck. A shadow circled him, edging closer and closer and he waited for it to swallow him, but it didn't. It never did.

"Just take me!" he yelled at the apparition. "Stop tormenting me with threats of death! Reaper, do what you've come to do and take me, and let me have peace."

The reaper responded with an exit.

Bastian leaned against the leg of the piano and wept.

# CHAPTER 13

# OCTAVIAN

O ctavian Zane hadn't stepped foot in New Orleans in fifty years, give or take. He'd rather be in Rome or Paris or Dubai. It's not that he didn't like New Orleans. He liked it just fine. He just didn't like being reminded of his past. He didn't like being reminded of the one thing that could destroy his immortality.

He touched the strand of gray hair that had instigated this homecoming. It was a nuisance, a smudge on his otherwise flawless appearance. He would get it taken care of. All it would take was a visit to Juleanne Barbot's shop and then he could go back to life as usual.

A lot of the Crescent City had changed over the years, but only marginally. Octavian took the same streets that he'd walked in the twenties, turned the same corner, and strolled down the same back alley to find a glass door that was as old as he was. The shop seemed to have had a new paint job recently, changing its wooden trim from red to black. He turned the knob and pushed it open. It still stuck and scuffed the wooden floor.

Stepping foot inside was like stepping back in time. The walls were the same dark teal green. The same spices and herbs lined tall shelves in mismatched jars. It even smelled like it had the very first time he ever set foot inside to meet Juleanne Barbot; smoke and sage with a hint of bergamot.

"Can I help you?" A young woman, her skin a little smoother and lighter than her great grandmother's, with deep brown eyes, and black curls tucked into a bright scarf atop her head, looked every bit of Juleanne. She wiped her hands on a black apron as she entered from the back room.

"Good morning, miss, I'm Octavian Z..."

"I know who you are," she cut off his introduction and scowled.

Octavian swallowed down a biting remark and exchanged it for a sweet smile and saccharine words that he hoped would charm her enough to get the help he needed. "And I know who you are as well, Meg. Your great-grandmother was a friend of mine."

"I don't think that's the way she saw it."

"Perhaps you are correct. Maybe colleagues would be a better term. The point is, she helped me once and I find myself in need of the same kind of help again." Octavian stepped closer to the front counter.

Meg pressed her brown hands on the edge of the counter and stared at him. Her gaze felt like fire, burning holes in his skin and soul. It made Octavian uncomfortable, and he didn't like feeling uncomfortable. "It's fading, the link between you and whatever poor soul you swindled a century ago." She waved her hand toward his hair.

"It appears so, yes. I assume you can do all the same wondrous things your grandmother, Juleanne, was able? Restore the link?"

"I don't do what Grandmama did," Meg said. "And I doubt aromatherapy is going to fix this for you."

Octavian scoffed. "No, I doubt it would. But I am willing to bet some knowledge got passed down that would be a bit more helpful." Octavian cooled his voice, biting the last words. He wanted this exchange to go smoothly. The fuss of being threatening was tiring and he would rather not have to go that route.

Meg swallowed, seeming to understand. She reached under the counter and pulled out a leather-bound book full of old pieces of scribbled paper. "I need to see exactly what Grand-mama did. Give me a minute."

"Take whatever time you need," Octavian replied. "I'll wait." He stepped across the room and took a seat at a wooden table covered in drippings of candle wax. He pulled out his pocket watch to find it still ticking. Not that he was surprised. He had looked at the watch a thousand more times since that moment in Rome. Its hands still pushed forward and pushed him further back to mortality.

Exactly thirty-seven minutes and fifteen seconds passed while Octavian waited for Meg to find the answers she needed. He heard the book close behind him in a shuffle of pages. "So, then…" he turned to face Meg.

She stepped from behind the counter, carrying the book with her, and joined him across the table. "Grandmama did deep magic to help you. Strong, dark magic, unlike anything she did for anyone else."

"What can I say? Juleanne and I had an arrangement. She helped me and I helped her. She felt it was worth the risk."

"How exactly did you help her?" Meg leaned close and raised an eyebrow.

"I'm surprised no one ever told you." Octavian put his watch away and leaned back in his chair. "Your grandfather was young and *somehow* got himself into trouble—the kind of trouble where one ends up hanging from trees—and he needed some help getting out of it. I was happy to assist in exchange for…"

"I'm sure you were." A tear left the corner of Meg's eye and rolled down her cheek. She wiped it away and straightened her shoulders like she was trying to appear unafraid of him.

But Octavian noticed the twitch of her jaw. It was good for

her to be afraid. He was a terrible adversary whose help could turn to hurt in a blink.

"Every curse has a lock that binds it. And with every lock comes a key," Meg averted her eyes as she spoke.

"And Bas…the tethered soul? He has this key?" It was unfathomable. How and where would he even begin to piece together the information that he would need for such a task? Octavian had been very careful to keep him in the dark on the details for this very reason.

"No, I doubt he even knows there is a key given Grandmama's notes. But that doesn't mean the key can't find its way to him. It's the way of things when the Higher Power wishes to tip the scales, restore something stolen."

"Higher Power?" Octavian laughed. No power ever cared enough about him or Bastian Roux. "Nothing was stolen, my dear. It was all freely given."

"That may be how it appeared at the time, but right now something is moving that key closer to whoever you linked yourself to, and the closer it gets, the weaker the bonds of this curse become."

"Then I find the key and I destroy it?"

"You can try. If the key is a thing, you might get lucky. But if it's a person…"

"Person?"

"Great grandmama's notes say part of her spell was the tears of a newly broken heart, which means that the key could be a person. But she also mentions a ring and…"

"The ring." Octavian breathed the word like a secret long forgotten. Bastian's ring. A piece of him that Juleanne needed, a piece he had stolen. "I gave the ring to Juleanne. Where is it now?"

"You think I still have a ring she used to build a curse a hundred years ago?" Meg laughed. "You're lucky I still have her journal after a hundred years. Hurricane Katrina…"

Octavian growled and pounded his fist on the table. It shook so hard that the jars across the room rattled from the wake.

"Calm down now," Meg soothed. "Something like that she wouldn't have kept here. It would be too powerful. She would have hidden it, buried it away for safekeeping."

"Where?"

"I don't know, but I can probably find out." Meg flipped through the book again. "If it's not in here, there are other journals we salvaged. Or at least pieces of them. I can talk to some family, maybe. It'll just take a little time."

Octavian smoothed his hair back and took a deep breath to smooth his anger into a facade of calm. "Find it…soon."

"I will," Meg replied. "And in the meantime, if I were you, I'd find out what your friend has been up to."

"Up to? Bastian?" Octavian was amused by the notion of Bas doing anything but sulking in his theater. "He lives between worlds. He can't do much of anything, my dear."

"Then you have nothing much to worry about." Meg stood up to walk away.

Octavian grabbed her wrist and twisted it just enough to get her full attention. "Let's hope not."

# CHAPTER 14
# ODETTE

Odette needed coffee. And beignets. And to go back to a time before she could see dead people. Well, before she could see *one* dead person. She was most definitely not suited to go all ghost whisperer for a whole city of spirits. She wasn't even really cut out to help trolley-guy cross over, or follow the light, or take care of his unfinished business, or whatever one did for ghosts.

"Hey, darlin'," Lizzie smiled from behind the counter, her voice soothing to Odette's soul. "The usual?"

"Yes! Large. And a bag of those fried pieces of heaven you call beignets." Odette leaned her elbows on the counter like it was a chore to hold herself up.

Lizzie slapped her hip and threw her head back and laughed. "I knew you'd get hooked on my beignets. Joe! Fry up some fresh ones for Odette." She started making Odette's latte. "Rough day? You look like you've seen a ghost."

"Ha!" The laugh jumped out of Odette's mouth before she even knew it was coming. "If only you knew," she replied, counting her words. While seeing Bastian up close and personal proved to her she wasn't losing her mind, she was still pretty sure the story wouldn't have the same effect on anyone else.

"Well, whatever it is that happened, you look like you need this, so it's on the house." Lizzie handed over a steaming mocha.

"You don't have to do that...again." Odette took the cup and sipped it carefully.

"Nonsense, that's what community does, helps each other." She reached over the counter and patted Odette's arm just as Joe stepped in from the back with a brown bag in his hand. Lizzie took it and passed it over to Odette. "You may not be near family, but that doesn't mean you don't have family here."

"I appreciate that," Odette replied. "Really." She felt tears rising and a lump forming in her throat.

"Good, now get out of here and go get some rest." Lizzie smiled big and handed her a napkin. "Enjoy those beignets before they get cold."

"Will do." Odette lifted her cup in salute before turning to head home.

She dabbed the napkin under her eyes as she stepped out onto the sidewalk. It had been a trying afternoon, and thanks to this small gesture of kindness and hospitality, she felt at least a bit cared for so far away from home. If the feeling was nice, why was she crying? It was probably a mix of homesickness and loneliness and getting yelled at by ghost-boy. But whatever the reasons, she would not give Bastian Roux the satisfaction of making her cry even if he couldn't see the tears.

At home, Odette dropped her keys and purse on the counter, kicked her shoes off, and plopped onto the sofa. Her mocha had cooled enough to abandon small sips in exchange for a larger swallow, after which she set the cup down, pulled a beignet out of the bag and promptly stuffed it into her mouth. Powdered sugar blew off her lips and onto her shirt like a dusting of fine snow. Her cheeks were so full she could barely muster the room to chew. But it tasted so good.

With a long and soulful meow, Hepburn jumped onto the couch and crawled across her chest, sniffing sugar residue as she went. She nuzzled Odette's face, then meowed again.

"Don't you start with me," Odette managed to mumble through a still-stuffed mouth. "You've been home alone for all of two hours, if that."

Hepburn meowed again and hopped off Odette's stomach to stretch and then curled up beside her on the couch.

Odette scratched the cat's head. "I would have been better off if I had stayed with you."

Hepburn purred.

"Who needs to worry about a trolley-guy from a ghost story, anyway? I let my curiosity get the better of me and you know what they say about curiosity, don't you?" She glanced at Hepburn, who was beginning to sweetly snooze. "Well, let's just say it and cats don't go well together." Odette bit into another beignet and then chased it with another chug of her latte.

"I don't even know why I went in the first place." She continued her rant, knowing the cat never really cared to begin with. "What did I expect to happen? Did I think we were just going to have a chat over tea?" She slouched further into the sofa. "I blame the music. If I had never heard that darn music, I wouldn't be in this predicament." She stroked Hepburn's soft fur. "And the nun!" She sat up and startled the cat, who growled under its breath before settling back to sleep.

"I mean, if she hadn't been all cryptic and weird about the whole thing, I probably would have left well enough alone." Odette took another bite of the beignet. "And if she knew ghost-boy could be all temperamental, then she could have offered to go with me and make a proper introduction. Then maybe things wouldn't have gone south like they did, and I wouldn't have ended up with heart palpitations and sweaty armpits."

Odette needed to calm down. She needed to stop her ranting and just pet the cat and let her fried nerves settle. She'd gone. She'd seen. She'd ran. She'd gotten coffee. It was over. Now to stop thinking about Bastian Roux. "How dare he scare me the way he did!"

Hepburn had apparently had enough and jumped off the couch and sauntered toward the kitchen.

"It was rude, Hepburn, that's what it was...rude." Odette looked over her shoulder to keep talking to the cat who didn't care. "*He's* the ghost. He should understand how people would feel when they see him and not be so creepy and terrifying. It isn't every day a person meets a ghost."

*And maybe it isn't every day that ghost-boy gets visitors.*

Odette didn't like that last thought. Sympathy came with it, and she didn't want to sympathize or empathize or anything else with Bastian. But she'd thought the thought and now she couldn't help but wonder what he must have felt having someone see him. Sister Mary Cecilia acted like that was highly unusual and she herself couldn't see him, only hear him. Why could Odette see him?

"No, no, no." She laid her head back against the couch and closed her eyes. "Don't start asking questions again, Odette. Just let this go."

*You strike me as the type of person that doesn't let things like this go.*

That sister and her words were coming back to bite Odette on the rear end. The nun had been right, of course. She didn't let things go. Not things like this. She'd read too much Nancy Drew and watched too much Scooby-Doo as a kid. But this mystery was looking less and less the kind where you pull a mask off of old Mr. Jenkins and realize it was just a trick and not a real spirit. But still, she couldn't let this go. Anxiety, curiosity, and a hint of compassion were combatting her best efforts.

What did she know? Bastian Roux was a jazz musician in the twenties who disappeared and was presumed dead. People say they hear him, or what they assume to be him, playing music in the old theater. The nun corroborated this story because she can hear the music and apparently can talk to Bastian. Odette also hears the music, and she can hear Bastian. She can also see him

—what there was of him to see. Why? That was the million-dollar question.

Odette's inner monologue started to sound like an old detective movie, and she needed to stop. She needed to sleep. She needed to find out why this was all happening.

"What? No!" She stood up and shook her head at her own thoughts. "I don't need to find out anything because I don't need this in my life."

Hepburn returned and rubbed against Odette's leg, meowing.

"Don't argue with me," Odette replied to the cat. "I'm not Jennifer Love Hewitt."

Another meow.

"You don't know that," she retorted and scooped the cat into her arms. "My seeing him doesn't mean I can help him, or that I should help him." What kind of help could he need?

The nun was right. She most definitely, contrary to her desire, was not capable of letting this go; not without more information and one more good try, at least. Odette was a person who believed in something greater than herself. She couldn't imagine a world in which this was happening without a reason. She couldn't live with herself if there was a tortured soul out there needing her help. Even if that tortured soul was a very rude ghost-boy whom she didn't like very much at the moment.

# CHAPTER 15
# ODETTE

Odette's alarm clock ticked closer and closer to seven a.m. She'd barely slept thinking about Bastian and destiny and everything in between. A couple of times she almost talked herself back out of having any more to do with him, but then that nagging idea that there was a sort of reason, plan, or providence behind all of this pulled her back in.

Her alarm bell finally rang, clanging metal that made the little mint-green clock jump and dance along the top of her nightstand. She slapped a hand to turn it off and grumbled under her breath.

Hepburn echoed her grumble with a little, throaty growl from where she lay at Odette's feet.

"I share the feeling," Odette said to the cat as she sat up and stretched her arms over her head. She arched her back to loosen tight muscles. The wood floor was cold on the bottoms of her bare feet. She shuffled quickly to the bathroom, but the tile floor was even colder. So was the water she splashed on her face. The chill made her skin go pink and helped her senses clear.

Odette had just a couple hours before the bookstore opened, so she rushed to get dressed, grabbing a floral frock from her tiny closet, hoping it wasn't too wrinkled. Louisiana was warmer than Virginia, but still chilly enough this time of year to warrant a cardigan and some tights before pulling on her brown oxfords and throwing her hair into a messy bun. There was no time for makeup or contacts. Just her glasses and the same necklace she always wore and her favorite ring, the one that had been her grandmother's. It was like a talisman that made her feel connected to loved ones.

Hepburn meowed at the bedroom door.

"Coming," Odette replied. She rushed to the kitchen to feed the cat and grab her purse. She really needed to figure out how to program her coffee maker because she didn't have time to brew a pot. Madame Clary's it was…again.

"I'll be back tonight." Odette grabbed her purse and keys from where she'd left them the night before and was out the door and making her way to The Castle Rose theater.

The stop for coffee had been a quick one. It was Lizzie's morning rush, so the cafe owner had little time for more than a quick greeting between taking orders. Odette was a bit thankful for that as she laid a five-dollar bill on the counter and scooted out. She was sure she looked worse than the previous evening and wasn't prepared to give Lizzie a reason for the dark circles under her eyes. She was also sure the look Lizzie had given her meant there would be questions and conversation the next time Odette stopped in. She wouldn't have better answers later, but a little time might cheer her complexion and stave off further concern. Not that she didn't appreciate that there was someone who worried about her. Odette didn't make friends easily and had no explanation for why or how this woman had become a friend so quickly, except that it had to be something in the way Lizzie was wired, because it was certainly not in Odette's nature. But this morning wasn't the time to analyze it all. This morning she had a mission.

Odette proceeded down the street and into the abbey court-yard. The gate squeaked when she opened it; she made a mental note to bring a can of oil next time.

"Good morning," Sister Mary Cecilia greeted from the little garden by the abbey doors.

"Are you always out here?" Odette asked. She hadn't meant it to come out as rude as it sounded, but lack of sleep meant her verbal filter was on the fritz.

The sister laughed. "Usually. I like being outdoors. Gardening makes me feel closer to the Maker." She stood up, wiping her hands on the apron that was tied around her waist. "I'm a little surprised to see you back here, though."

"I'm not the type to let things go, remember?"

"Oh, that I believe," Sister Mary Cecilia chuckled. "I just thought it'd take you until this evening."

"Apparently I'm more tenacious than that."

"A little tenacity might be just the trick." The nun reached into the pocket of her tunic and pulled out the same skeleton key from the day before. She handed it to Odette. "I have morning prayers, so just hide it under that blue flowerpot when you're done."

"I will." Odette took the rusty key. "Thank you."

The nun smiled and nodded before grabbing her basket of fresh herbs and going inside.

Odette looked at the key. She turned it over in her hand. It was cold. Heavier than she thought. Suddenly, the whole thing felt heavy. Was she really going to go back in there? Was she going to face him again? Odette squared her shoulders. She was. And this time, there would be no running away from his bark or bite. Not until she had some answers.


The morning sun made the theater brighter than the day before. Tiny particles floated in the beams of light filtering through the windows like fairy dust. The crystal light fixtures glinted and glittered. Odette could better see the embossed gold of the wall-paper peeling off the walls. The broken vase had been cleaned off the stage floor and the roses lay wilting on top of the piano.

She set her latte down and picked up one of the blooms, holding it to her nose. The sweetness tickled her nostrils.

A noise echoed from somewhere behind her.

Odette's nerves came to attention. Goosebumps followed the shiver that made her feel cold under her cozy sweater. "I know you're here."

Silence.

Odette turned around, looking for some sign of Bastian. "I'm not leaving this time...Bastian." Though in truth, she was secretly counting down, and if there was no response in seven more seconds, she was actually leaving.

A trickle of music flowed from the piano.

Odette startled. "If you go all music of the night, I may change my mind."

"I doubt I'd be so lucky," Bastian spoke from behind the piano keys. He looked exactly the same as before. Not that he would look different. Unless ghosts can change clothes, which Odette doubted.

"I appreciate sarcasm." Odette traded the rose for her latte. "Moreso than being scared to death."

"You look very much alive to me..." He paused and looked at her with a raised brow.

"If this is your way of apologizing and asking my name, it's Odette. Odette Durand." She sipped the latte, her nose scrunching as she realized it had gone lukewarm.

"I was aware of your name...Odette." Bastian's mouth softened as he whispered the last word, her name. His eyes gazed into hers like he could read beneath her surface.

Odette squirmed under his stare.

He cast his eyes back down toward the piano. "Why did you come back?"

"Why can I see you?"

"I have no idea," he responded as his fingers piddled between two notes. "Sister Mary Cecilia seems to think it's because you can break this curse."

"Curse?" In all her processing and ranting and wondering, Odette had never truly considered the prospect of a curse as legitimate, no matter how often it was mentioned in the stories. "Can ghosts even be cursed?" That question was meant more for herself than for Bastian.

"I'm not a ghost."

"Excuse me?" His response caught up to Odette's thoughts and she resisted laughing. "If it looks like a ghost and acts like a ghost and died a hundred years ago…see where I'm going with this? I mean, you can live in denial all you want, but the chances aren't in your favor, ghost-boy."

"While I very much get the insinuation on your part…" Bastian looked at his torso and hands, "given that I'm less than fully corporeal, I did not die a hundred years ago. No dying means no ghost. Or so I've been told."

"Then what are you?"

"No one…nothing." His head bowed lower, and his shoulders slunk down to match the somber tone that deflated his voice. "Nothing at all."

He was no beast, after all. Right now, he wasn't frightening in the slightest. But he did seem frightened. Or tired. Or just very sad. Odette took another sip of her latte, hoping the few seconds would allow her an extra moment with which to dig up some courage. Then she stepped around the side of the piano to take a seat on the bench next to Bastian. "If you are no one and nothing, then I am crazy, and I refuse to believe I am crazy."

"You can live in denial if you want," Bastian replied, and the slightest smirk curled one corner of his lips upward.

Odette laughed. "Ghost-boy has jokes."

"Not a ghost. And certainly not a boy."

"What? You want me to call you *ghost-man*?" Odette gagged. "That sounds like a character in a Top Gun movie which doesn't feel like your vibe."

"Top Gun?" Bastian asked.

"You've been hanging around with nothing to do for a

century and you don't hop into the cinema for a show every once in a while? I'd live at the movies."

"I've seen movies," Bastian retorted. "It's just been a while."

"Obviously," Odette chuckled. "But movie references aside, I'm sticking with ghost-boy."

"Fine, but I'm still not a ghost."

Odette still wasn't so sure about that. "If you didn't die, what happened to you?"

Bastian banged the keys, and it made her jump a little. He ran his fingers through his hair, making his curls twist and topple. "I was selfish and afraid. I sold my soul to the devil in exchange for a trick."

"Like the actual devil?" Odette quirked an eyebrow.

"No," Bastian scoffed. "But a close second. Someone I thought was a friend made me an offer I should have refused. Dying as I should have, leaving Catherine the way I was meant to, it all would have been a cheaper price than trying to cheat death. I ended up being the one cheated, and it's my own fault."

"Who's Catherine?"

"A girl I loved once. I was going to marry her. I broke her heart just to save myself." Odette swore a tear was teetering at the edge of Bastian's lashes. Could ghosts cry?

"I don't understand," she whispered.

"Voodoo, love," Bastian replied to her unspoken questions. "Or hoodoo, I always get the two confused. The point is, I didn't want to die. Someone told me they could stop death if I broke Catherine's heart, so I did. And I found myself to be just a pawn in their bid for immortality. They cursed me to live between worlds so they could live forever." Bastian stood up. "I have no one to blame but myself."

Odette sipped her latte while watching as Bastian paced the length of the grand piano. He was sarcastic, which she kind of liked, but he was also a defeatist, which she didn't like. Part of her wanted to scold him and tell him to buck up buttercup; that he'd made a bad call once, and he needed to get over it. But this wasn't choosing the wrong major in college or getting engaged to the wrong guy. This was much larger and there was no moving on. Her heart broke a little for him in that regard. He was trapped. She knew what that felt like. And even if it was in part to his selfishness and fear, he should have a chance at freedom.

"I want to help you."

Bastian paused and stared at her. "What?"

The admission surprised Odette as much as it had Bastian. She was conceding to every argument she'd had with herself since she'd first heard the music. But she knew this wasn't how anyone should live...even century-old sort-of-dead piano players.

"I want to help you," Odette repeated, standing. "I mean, I've read enough books and seen enough movies to know that curses can be broken, right?"

Bastian sniggered. "You can't help me, not with this. No one can."

"No one could see you until me either, but here we are, so how about we put that 'can't' word away for a minute? I'm pretty persistent, ghost-boy."

"Not a ghost."

"Not the point." Odette pushed her glasses up her nose. "If you were cursed, then let's find a way to break it." She chugged the last bit of her cold mocha.

"Like in the movies?" Bastian questioned. "So what, you kiss me like some princess charming?"

Odette almost spit out her coffee. "Whoa there, I don't kiss guys I just met, ghost-boy."

"Not a ghost," he reminded her. "But why? Why do this for me?"

Odette looked at him with her mouth open, expecting a witty retort to emerge, but there was only silence. She closed her mouth and considered the question...considered the reason. She believed in providence. She believed she was here and could see

Bastian for a reason. But it was more than that. "I didn't find out I was dyslexic until high school," she said.

Bastian's brow wrinkled with an expression of confusion.

When Odette was first diagnosed, she had done all kinds of research on the subject, including its history. It was quite possible Bastian hadn't ever heard that term when he was alive.

"You might know it as, 'word blindness.' It has to do with how your brain processes the words that it reads. The very simplified version is your eyes read the words, but your brain mixes up the letters."

Bastian nodded.

Odette took a breath and continued. "Most of my school years before that diagnosis were a struggle. What came so easily to other kids was really hard for me. I felt stupid. I was different and didn't understand why." Odette paused. She glanced at Bastian, who was waiting for her to continue with soft eyes. "When your brain doesn't work like everyone else's, it's easy to let yourself fade into the background. I moved to the back of the classrooms; the edges of the playgrounds…mostly by myself. I felt hopeless and obscured. So I guess I just know what it feels like to be invisible, and I know that it's pretty crummy."

"It is," Bastian said.

"For a long time, dyslexia was like my own little curse. Learning it had a name—finding help—broke it. Maybe you just need some help to break your curse. Why not me?" Odette dared another peek at Bastian whose misty eyes were locked with hers. Warmth blushed her cheeks. She adjusted her slipping glasses. "Well…" She pulled her phone out of her purse to check the time. "I've got to get to work. But we aren't done, you and I."

"I suppose I have no say in this," Bastian said, his voice sounding suddenly dry.

Odette was already walking away. She waved her hand, physically brushing off the notion. "Not really."

She didn't even glance back. She had set her mind on helping Bastian Roux break this curse, and that was what she was going to do, whether he liked it or not. She was now fully convinced of her ramblings. Nothing happened without a reason. If she could see him, then she could help him. If she was the only one who could see him, perhaps she was the only one who could help him be seen.

# CHAPTER 16

# OCTAVIAN

Octavian sat on a bench across the street from the theater. The building had aged in the years since he had last lain eyes on it. Cracks in the brick. More windows were boarded up than not across the front. Anywhere else in the world and some developer would have razed it to the ground and built something new. This city paid homage to ghosts though, and so a once beautiful theater had dilapidated into nothing more than Bastian Roux's tomb. One complete with flowers to mark the grave.

The wall overgrown with roses was a bit of a curiosity to Octavian. This time of year, the emerging blooms should still be hidden. Yet here they were, painted with the blood-red of summertime. Most would find them beautiful in contrast to the dying building. They only nauseated him. He liked beautiful things, but he loathed Bastian. He hated that, like those roses, he was life forever connected to death. He could feel it, their connection, like a string, pulled taut the closer he was to Bastian's presence. It's why he kept his distance. Oh, to be free of this place and that feeling once again.

The faint notes of the piano filtered from the theater. Just a few and they stopped. Silence. Then a banging minor chord. More silence.

Octavian smirked at the tortuous echo. He stood just as a trolley came to a stop, waiting until the unloading passengers cleared and the vehicle moved on before he moved to cross the street and confront his past. Just as his feet hit the opposite sidewalk, he saw a figure emerge from a back doorway that was almost covered by greenery. He tucked himself against a lamppost and observed a young woman lock the door. She pushed her glasses up on her nose, then looked at the key in her hand and smiled before hiding it under a flowerpot closer to the abbey.

Octavian watched her walk away. What business would she have in that theater?

*Something is moving that key closer to whoever you linked yourself to and the closer it gets, the weaker the bonds...* He cursed under his breath. Could this girl be the key? Could she have it?

Octavian wasn't taking any chances. He turned on his heel and headed deeper into the Quarter, toward Barbot's shop.

"I hope that you have answers for me this morning," Octavian said, stepping through the black door.

"I don't." Meg lit a candle and set it on the counter.

Octavian's jaw clenched. "You are far too calm given that response, my dear."

"It is the only response I have."

He looked her over, up and down, glaring into her unwavering eyes. "You are a lot like her. Juleanne edged too close to the line herself...poking at my patience. It almost cost your great-grandmother her son."

He watched Meg's throat dip as she swallowed.

He smiled at her and reached his hand to touch hers. "We should be friends, you and I."

She pulled away from his grasp. "I'll find your key."

"I have no doubt, but I need it now." Octavian could feel his body weakening. Muscles ached and bones cracked in ways they hadn't before. Age was catching up with him and he would not sit and wait for it to devour him.

"Grandmama mentioned the ring, but not what it looks like and not where she put it. I've read all her journals, looked through boxes, and still have plenty more to search."

"It is a gold signet ring with a rose etched into it." Octavian offered the description. "Is there a chance someone else could have the ring?"

Meg raised an eyebrow. "Someone else like who?"

"Like a girl, a young girl."

"I doubt it," Meg replied. "Grandmama took her work seriously and protected it from those who could misuse it or undo it. That ring will be wherever she left it and that would not have been where another soul could easily get hands on it."

"You are certain?" Octavian touched a hand to the fold of his jacket, feeling the tick of his watch from within.

"I am, but you must think this girl means something?"

"You said the key was being moved closer, that it could even be a person?"

"It's possible, but that wouldn't be my first concern. Knowing Grandmama…"

"Well, I am looking into all areas of concern and there is a girl who seems to be tiptoeing too near to all of this, and whoever she is, I won't be undone by her." Octavian's heart pumped harder inside his chest and the top of his head grew warm.

Meg inched backward. "What makes you think she truly has anything to do with this?"

"Let's just say she was in very close proximity to my tethered soul, too close." Octavian spun around to pace across the shop. He had very little real information and could be jumping into the deep end of conclusions, but something about her smile had given him great pause. "I don't trust that proximity. It means something and I will find out what. Perhaps I should just kill her."

"You would kill an innocent soul?"

"Innocent?" Octavian turned to see Meg's shocked expression at his outburst. He smoothed his hair back into place and noticed a photo in a gold frame—Meg holding a little boy. He picked up the picture and traced a finger over the cheerful child's face. "No one is innocent." He smashed the object, shattering the glass before dropping it to the floor. "And yes, I would kill her without hesitation if it meant my security."

Meg's hand trembled, and her voice matched. "I wouldn't advise it."

"Good thing I'm not asking for your advice."

"Curses are tricky things and what you think is the right step could be the exact thing that undoes it all." She swallowed again. "If the girl is the key, or more likely has something to do with the key, killing her could be just the twist that opens the lock. So if you want to kill her, go ahead, but it might be better to watch her, keep her away from your poor soul, and give me time to understand exactly how Grandmama's curse works."

"Time is something I find myself in short supply of these days." Shards crackled under Octavian's feet as he returned to the counter and leaned over it, his face so close to Meg's he felt her rapid breath against his cheeks. Despite her effort to pull away again, he took her by the hands and squeezed her fingers. "I suggest you work quickly at understanding all this, or my patience may run out." He glanced at the broken image behind him, then back to her tense expression. "Your son has your eyes."

"You need me," Meg replied through gritted teeth. Tears escaped down her cheeks.

He squeezed her tighter. "I don't need you. There's a shop like yours with a woman like Juleanne around every corner of this city and more in the bayou. If you can't figure this out, I am sure one of them can." He released her hands.

She pulled them to her chest and massaged her fingers. "I'll find out what you need."

"Good girl," Octavian smiled. "I'm going to keep a close eye on this little whoever-she-is that is sniffing around my soul, and you are going to get my answers and we will all live happily forever after." He retrieved the damaged photograph and tossed it onto the counter.

Meg jumped.

Octavian laughed as he walked back outside, his mind musing with ways to keep Bastian in his place, to keep himself alive. He wasn't about to let some petite librarian or second-rate voodoo queen ruin him.

# CHAPTER 17

# ODETTE

O dette sat at a table in the middle of the bookshop with a stack of books and a notepad in front of her. The story-time children laughing at Isabelle's antics in the back corner offered a jovial soundtrack to her studying of much darker, more uncomfortable things.

Odette had pulled every book the shop had that spoke of voodoo and hoodoo and curses. She reheated her second latte twice while reading through line after line of book after book. She was taking a crash course on the subject; searching for anything which might help her help Bastian. While she hadn't expected to find a copy of *How to Break Curses for Dummies*, it would have been nice. Even just a chapter or section that gave a step-by-step guide. Would that be too much to ask?

Five books in, and Odette didn't have any answers. She came to understand that curses were secret things. They were hushed whispers more than loud shouts, pinpricks rather than gunshots. They were each as unique and personal as the practitioner who created them and the purpose of their creation. There wouldn't be any three-step, generic solution to this problem. So, Odette opened another book and read another line, and then another, and then another.

"See you next week!" Isabelle called after the small herd of laughing children stampeding through the shop, followed by parents carrying jackets and half-full paper cups of goldfish crackers.

Odette shut her notebook, readying herself to step away from her mission and return to her actual job.

"Don't stop on my account." Isabelle picked up a book, flipping through the pages.

"I'm sorry," Odette replied. "We were slow, so I thought…"

"You are fine, dear." Isabelle patted her shoulder and then took a seat across the table. "Never apologize for reading. Besides, we are slow today and you look rather engrossed in this topic." She quickly perused the spines of Odette's haphazard book stack. "Voodoo? Taking another step into the more supernatural cultural elements of our fair city?"

"Something like that," Odette replied. "I guess you could say the ghost stories started me on a path." She didn't want to lie. But she couldn't yet divulge the full truth.

Isabelle arched an eyebrow but didn't push for more detail, even if she suspected there was more to this new hobby than simple curiosity. "Well, hopefully you will find what you're looking for." She patted the cover of one book and then got up. "I need a cup of tea." Then she was off to the back.

Odette sipped her latte—which was already cold again—and reached for the book Isabelle had looked at. The woman's gesture probably wasn't meant to be any sort of inclination, but she had nothing more concrete to go on anyway, so she went with it.

This book, it turned out, was more of the same history and mythos as all the others. She skimmed its pages in hopes of something more tangible. Then paused as she suddenly found a notion she could latch onto. About ten chapters in, she hit a sort of listing, or more like a lineage, of the voodoo queens of the French Quarter from the 1800s onward. She'd already read enough to know that, if anyone could do it, these were the women who had the influence and the means to create the kind of curse that could trap a man between worlds for a century. Perhaps if she could find the right practitioner, she could find more details that would lead to breaking Bastian's curse. But why would anyone want to do this to another person? What could Bastian Roux have done to make someone this angry with him?

They were valid questions because, from everything Odette read, along with her movie and tv-based knowledge of such things, a curse like this wasn't just thrown around for no good reason. If it was money, there might be a trail because it would have to be a lot of money. Other motives would be harder to pin down.

Revenge was a possibility. Bastian had mentioned breaking some girl's heart. But that was *after* making a deal with the devil, so did it fit the timeline that said girl would have this done to him? Maybe it was a rival like the ghost stories claimed. But he said he made a deal to save his own life. From what? From who? Who was the devil that Bastian had made a deal with? Maybe that connection would lead Odette in the right direction.

When did she start sounding like a private detective? Ugh. Odette liked a cheesy P.I. flick, but she didn't want to be one. She needed to get a grip on her internal voice with all this. And she would need to talk to Bastian again. There must be more to the story and perhaps, in the case of curses at least, the devil really was in the details.

Odette rolled her eyes at herself and grabbed her latte to reheat it one last time in hopes of actually finishing it before the day was over. She figured she had about as much chance of succeeding at that task as she did at figuring out this whole curse thing in one day, but she wasn't going to let a good latte go to waste without a fight. She wasn't going to give up on Bastian without one, either. We all need someone to fight for us, and she had been feeling a little feistier lately.

CHAPTER 18

# BASTIAN

There was a time when Bastian would sleep in and spend his afternoon walking around the city, planning his set list for that night's performance at The Castle Rose. He'd missed rehearsals with the band and dinners at Catherine's house, with her mother eyeing him warily from her end of the table because she'd never trusted musicians. He remembered laughing, and he remembered what it felt like to be alive. For the first time in a very long time, he thought about being alive; sweat on your brow, holding hands, dancing to a happy song, that kind of alive.

His fingers tickled the piano keys, putting together a tune he hadn't played in a long time. He let his foot tap along to the jazzy tempo. He let a smile creep along his face and seep beneath his skin into a deeper well—one long dry of joy. But as quickly as he let it all come swooping in, he cast it aside with a low chord and a growl. It was a bit of hope, and he'd almost swallowed it until the despair and doubt returned and swallowed him instead.

"Now why did you stop playing that song?" Sister Mary Cecilia's voice echoed across the stage as she entered, carrying her basket of roses.

Bastian didn't reply. Maybe if he was silent, she would think he'd retreated and leave him alone.

"I know you are still there, dearie." The nun dashed his hopes.

Bastian sighed. "I'm not in the mood for a merry song."

"You're never in the mood for a merry song and if you ask me, it's time for that to change. You are, altogether, too moody." The sister stopped at the piano and looked at the pile of crumpled, faded blooms left there to die. Her forehead wrinkled and her mouth drew downward in a frown that could only mean disappointment.

"I think I have earned the right to my solemn mood." Bastian closed the lid of the piano to cover the keys.

Sister Mary Cecilia jumped at the abrupt sound the lid made as it shut. "Solemn is a pleasant word for it, and whether one has the right to a mood or not doesn't mean it's the best thing for them. I think it is high time you chose to gift yourself with a little more joy."

"Joy? Ha! What joy is found in death?"

"You aren't dead." She set her basket on top of the grand piano. "Besides, joy isn't about the circumstance, it's about the perspective."

"From where I sit, the view is quite tragic."

"Sit somewhere else." Sister Mary Cecilia crossed her arms over her chest and glared in his direction with a raised eyebrow. "You are being given a gift and I fear if you don't see it for what it is, you will succumb fully to the darkness looking to destroy you."

"There is no gift for the likes of me, Sister. Hope is folly."

"Hope is never foolish." She went to work pulling supplies from her basket; a vase, a bottle of water, and fresh-cut flowers.

Bastian watched her trade out the dead blossoms for some full of color and life. She watered them and tended their space until they created a bright bouquet adorning his shadowed stage. "Why do you bring me flowers?"

Sister Mary Cecilia paused her arranging. "Because they are beautiful and can remind you that life isn't over. Even in the dead of winter, when the vines look lifeless, they are still very much alive with the hope of the coming spring."

Bastian stood and walked toward the nun and her bouquet. He touched a single velvet rose. "But you cut them from the vine and so, no matter how much care you give them, all the roses you bring into this theater eventually fade and die. What hope is in that?"

The sister inclined her thoughtful gaze back toward his voice. "You are not cut off from the vine, Bastian."

He watched a tear trace the wrinkles of her cheek. "I am fading. I can feel it."

"No." She wiped the droplet away with the back of her wrinkled and splotched hand. "No, you are on the cusp of freedom, of life anew. You just have to see it."

"You believe that girl will break this curse? But what if I don't deserve for it to be broken?"

"My dear boy, if we all only got what we deserved, there would be no hope for any of us." Sister Mary Cecilia's crinkled features curled into a wide smile that brightened her blue eyes.

Bastian turned away, a lump forming in his throat. "You keep talking of hope as though it's some magic pill to fix all our ailments."

"It's not magic, and it's not a solution. It's a faith that keeps us moving forward." She picked up her basket.

Bastian wanted to reply with a snicker or maybe even a shout, a scream at the notion of faith. He had lost that before he'd lost the life he knew. Perhaps if he had had more faith, he wouldn't have been in this position. But his fear had been stronger and had killed it. It had not even occurred to him that it could be revived. What would he even have faith in? God? Himself? Some girl? Faith for what? Freedom that the nun spoke of? Would that mean getting to live or simply getting to die?

"Are you still there?" The nun whispered.

"Yes," Bastian replied, slumping back down onto his piano bench.

"I know it is difficult. I know that faith and hope are not easy things when you can't see the light. But even when you can't see it, trust those who can."

"And you see this light?"

"Indeed, I do." The nun smiled again and Bastian perceived that the light she spoke of was beaming from her. "Give the girl a chance. Let yourself hope, even if just a little." The nun gave no time for a reply. "And think twice before breaking another one of my vases, dearie. Or a curse will become the least of your worries. See you or not, I can scold you."

Bastian chuckled.

Sister Mary Cecilia winked before turning to march off toward the back door.

He lifted the piano lid back up, revealing the dusty black and white keys where his soul lived; his tether to sanity. Bastian stretched his fingers and touched them to the ivory with caution. He wouldn't go back to the uptempo melody of moments before —of a lifetime before—but he didn't deluge into his normal tragic concerto, either. He played something new; something in between mirth and melancholy. He almost smiled at the progress of not letting himself fully drown in his sorrow, but rather felt he was just wading in the waters instead. But only almost, because the waters were still there, and he wasn't yet ready to fully come onto the shore of hope.

# CHAPTER 19

# ODETTE

For the first time since starting her new job, Odette found herself counting down the minutes until closing time when she could see Bastian again and share her progress. Little as it was, it was better than nothing and offered questions that would perhaps get them moving in the right direction. It felt like a fire had been lit inside her and such silly things like missing facts and lacking details wouldn't douse it out. Those could be uncovered, especially now that she knew the right questions to ask.

"Hot date?" Isabelle grinned after ringing up the last customer.

Odette's cheeks warmed. "What? No. Just meeting a friend."

Isabelle nodded with her eyebrows and lips quirked in a way that looked more patronizing than convinced. "Well, don't let me keep you from something so exciting as to have your foot tapping."

Odette bit her lip and stopped her foot. "Oh no, I…uh…"

"Calm down, girl," Isabelle replied. "I didn't mean anything by it other than leaving work seven minutes and twenty-three seconds early isn't going to hurt anything. I have realized I would be lost without you, but that doesn't mean I can't close up myself now and again."

"Are you sure?" Odette felt bad.

"Positive. I won't be hanging around myself tonight either. I have my weekly card game to get to." Isabelle opened the cash register so she could pull the drawer and lock it away in the back safe. "Just lock the front door as you leave and flip the sign to say we're closed."

"Thank you, I will." Odette grabbed her coat and her purse, stuffing the book she had been studying inside.

Odette had packed a candle and matches in her bag, accounting for the absence of light in the theater. She set the little glass candle jar on the top of the piano. With a scratch and a sizzle, she lit the match and transferred the blaze to the candle's new wick. She waved her hand, and the match went out, leaving the smell of sulfur tickling her nose and mingling with the sweet jasmine being released by newly melting wax.

"Hey ghost-boy, you here?" Odette called into the dark behind the raggedy stage curtains. "Of course you are. Where else would you be?"

"Not a ghost, and I do go places." Bastian appeared near the piano like he was emerging from an invisible fog.

Odette noticed the way his arms swung at his sides as he sauntered to the bench. "Really? What places? I guess I did see you on the trolley that first time." She leaned her elbows on the piano.

"Why are you here? Again?" He wrinkled his brow, seemingly annoyed, but the left corner of his lips curled up just enough to negate the gesture.

Odette stood straight and dug for the book in her bag. "I've got some thoughts regarding your situation."

"Thoughts?" He tilted his head and arched one brow.

"Yes, thoughts. Nothing life-changing yet, but I've got a start." She flipped through the book, looking for the right page.

Bastian sighed. "You most definitely aren't going to let this go and leave me alone."

She only smiled at him in reply.

He chuckled. "So, where are we starting?"

Odette held up the book and tapped a finger toward the title. "Voodoo."

"Didn't we start there this morning?"

Odette ignored the hint of sarcasm in his tone and continued to flip pages. "Yes, but it was a very uneventful start and now I have a little more to go on. I've learned some things about voodoo." She found her page.

"One afternoon and you've learned things about voodoo. I'm all ears." He leaned back a bit and crossed his arms over his chest and smirked.

"Don't patronize me, ghost-boy. You said this was all some voodoo or hoodoo. I found a lead." She stuck her tongue out at him. He was not going to get under her skin and make her doubt her progress.

"Not a ghost, and what lead?" He sat up a little straighter.

She had piqued his interest. "Well, what little I could find on curses tells me that your curse is a big deal and not something that happens every day. So, I'm thinking not just anyone could have implemented said special curse."

"So, I'm special. Go on." He gestured for her to continue.

Odette rolled her eyes. "I'm thinking the only people who would have been able to handle this kind of curse were the voodoo queens...or kings?" She turned the book around, revealing the ancestry it held. "If I'm right, whoever did this to you went through one of them." The question of who would do this sprinted through her thoughts, followed closely by why they would want to hurt Bastian, which was just in front of the question of whether Bastian was the kind of guy that deserved it. She knew the answers would come, they would have to, but they weren't what mattered most at the moment.

From where Odette stood, the why behind the curse was less important than finding out who could have cast it. They were the key.

"Look, love," Bastian twitched and squirmed in his seat. "All that sounds smart and all, but I told you I stayed away from all that stuff. I was never told the details either, so I have no idea who the voodoo queens even were. It's not like they walked up and introduced themselves." He ran one hand over his transparent cheek and through his lopsided curls.

Odette pursed her lips and exhaled a short huff. "No, I guess they wouldn't have. But as I said, it's a start. Figuring out where the curse originated might help us understand it better and find a way to break it. It is a start, and a start is all I promised when I walked in here."

Bastian smiled, not a smirk, but a small grin that was equal parts sad and appreciative. "That it is, and that you did…Thank you." He paused before those last two words, glancing down at his hands.

It was a short beat, but Odette noticed it because, in that second of silent hesitation, something in the air shifted. There was a change in the weight and length and depth of the oxygen she was breathing. There was a new sweetness that wasn't from the candle that flickered next to her. "You're welcome," she replied. "I will keep looking."

"I have no doubt," he said, still not looking up from his hands.

Odette closed her book and set it on the piano. "So you go places, huh?"

"What?" Bastian looked up with a quirked brow.

"You said that you go places. What places?"

"Interested in a day in the life of a half-dead man?" He laughed, but it was more solemn than jovial.

"Well, maybe it will illuminate some vital information about our cause." Sure. That made sense. It was all for the sake of her mission. She returned the book to her purse. "Show me the places that mean something to you."

He looked away again with a sad shake of his head. "Very little means something to me after a century of entrapment."

The timbre of the last word, entrapment, cracked Odette's heart. She'd felt trapped once, imprisoned by the mirage of happiness she kept telling herself was real. If her ex hadn't broken up with her, she was sure she would have ended things with him in a month or three. She wouldn't have been able to take the suffocation of it longer than that. A century seemed too long a time to even fathom being unhappy. But she refused to believe all meaning was stolen away. One would have to hold on to something.

"This theater means something. It's home to you," she said. "So I'm sure there's at least one other spot in this big city that holds a place in that see-through heart of yours. I want to see it..." she picked up her purse and hung it from her shoulder, "...for research purposes."

Bastian stared at her. He squinted and sighed, then stood. "Alright...one place...for research purposes."

## CHAPTER 20
# BASTIAN

J ust before stepping out of the theater and into the night, Bastian stopped and turned to Odette. "Follow me, but also beware of talking to an invisible man while you walk down the street. People will think you're crazy."

"At this point, I'm fairly certain I am crazy," she replied without so much as a chuckle or stutter.

He led her through the nun's courtyard and down the avenue. It was dark but clear; the black sky shimmering with a million bright stars. They made him feel grounded. So many things had changed around him over the years, but not the stars. They looked just the same as they did when he was real.

Bastian walked with Odette beside him keeping pace with his long strides. She was close enough that he felt the warmth coming off her.

He tried not to give it more thought.

He *did* think about taking the trolley to their intended destination, but the night air was fresh, and perhaps this was less awkward than him trying not to get sat on while in Odette's company. He rather liked the normalcy of walking down the street with a girl.

"I used to live there," Bastian pointed to a faded brick

building with paint peeling from the window trim and chipping off the metal railing of the balconies. "In a one-room flat on the third floor."

Odette looked up and nodded but didn't say anything.

"It was nicer then." His mirage was broken by the combination of memory and the harsh reality of time wasted. Bastian put his hands in his pockets. One hundred years ago the building was new, and the paint was new; he was still new.

Bastian walked on, acknowledging a few points of interest from his past. He pointed to the diner where he used to eat breakfast on Monday mornings and told Odette how they'd made the eggs just the way he liked them, and the coffee was strong but not too strong. He mentioned the market where he'd always bought flowers for Catherine. Six pink tulips. But he couldn't bring himself to tell her that they were passing the street where Catherine had lived with her mother, and he dared not even think about turning right to walk in the direction of her former home. Not yet. Those memories weren't ready to be shared.

Odette nodded along with each offering, her smile all sweet, with no bitterness, unlike his own.

Bastian often ventured from the theater and walked down the street or rode the trolley while watching life in all its motion around him. When he did, it was impossible not to think of his past and all he had lost—all that he had missed out on, and all the pain he had caused.

This was not an odd occurrence. But it seemed different just now.

Perhaps Odette's company made it all the more real, the loss. Perhaps this new bit of hope flitting around his heart loosened and pulled at emotions that he had carefully tied away. He'd spent a century building up a resistance, or maybe more of a wall, and now it was toppling. Oh, there had always been pain, but it had grown stale in his years alone. Walking under the night sky with Odette made it all fresh again.

"You've gotten quiet," Odette whispered.

"Sorry," Bastian replied. He shook off his dreary thoughts and tried to put on a smile, but it wasn't enough to ease the concern from her features. "I'm fine," he tried again and almost meant it. While it grieved him to relive precious memories, there was also something very human and alive about sharing little pieces of himself with someone else.

Odette still didn't look convinced, but she nodded and turned her gaze back toward their walk.

The streets weren't overly crowded. Gathering clouds threatened rain, so maybe that was keeping people indoors. Bastian was glad it was sparse. It kept him from having to dodge unknowing passersby.

But not completely.

Turning a corner, an older gentleman walked right through him. He was accustomed to it and the strange sensation—like the pins and needles of a limb waking up—but it made Odette's breath catch.

"Does that happen often?"

"You get used to it." Bastian offered her another smile to ease the discomfort and pity scrunching her eyebrows.

They walked another few blocks in silence until the shops and homes which lined the streets were replaced by weeping willows and twisted oaks draped in Spanish moss.

Bastian remembered when they were barely more than saplings. They weren't so haunting back then.

"Just up ahead." He led Odette down a narrow path that followed a babbling creek and ended on a small stone bridge. "This is the spot."

Odette looked at him and then the bridge and the water and then back at him. He leaned on the bridge's low wall, and she stepped close to him and did the same. A breeze whispered by, carrying the lilac scent of her perfume. He liked the subtlety and sweetness of it.

"This place means something to you?" Odette asked. "What about it?"

"My mother was the only thing I regretted leaving behind when I came to America. Before I left, she gave me a ring. It had been her father's, just a little gold signet ring with a rose etched into it. The only thing of any value I had in this world. I treasured it because it reminded me of her. I needed those connections to her, to home. When I first came to New Orleans, I found this bridge, and it reminded me of her too. It was just like one we would picnic near when I was a boy. It was the first place that made this city feel like home. This is the place I would go to be alone, to think. To remind me of who I was...who I am."

Bastian gazed down at the water trickling over brown and gray rocks. The last rays of the setting sun danced on the surface of the soft current where tiny fish swam. They darted under roots that drank from the cool stream feeding large trees. The trees, Bastian thought, were eerily beautiful. They lined the bank and offered shade, making the place they were standing feel both hidden and haunting.

"And who are you exactly, Bastian Roux?" Odette asked, her head turning just enough to see him, to watch him with squinted eyes like she was weighing and measuring him.

"Now? I told you. Now I am nothing." He knew how depressed and defeated he sounded, but it was honest. To be more than nothing, one must do something that matters or be someone who matters to someone, and Bastian hadn't mattered in a long while.

Odette stood a little taller. Her face didn't move, but her eyes flitted up and down his length and he wasn't sure if she was considering him or her response.

"Then who were you?" She exhaled the question like a long breath.

Bastian inhaled and exhaled a deep breath of his own, giving himself a moment to remember the man he'd been, the one who seemed so foreign and strange to him now. "I was a nice guy, I guess. Happy to help a friend or neighbor. I was fun. I was the guy everyone came to hear on a Saturday night. The one who could get the whole crowd dancing or singing or laughing or crying. I was the one they wanted to have a drink with after my set." He turned his body toward Odette. "I was this guy from nowhere who got to do the thing he loved every day. I was happy. I was free. I was on the cusp of all my dreams coming true." He turned away from her and gazed back at the water rippling and rushing below them.

"Then why risk it all on a deal that cost your life?" Odette asked in little more than a whisper.

"I was already dying," Bastian replied.

"So, you tried to cheat death…" Odette's sentence faded off, and it was hard to tell if it was a question or just her repeating his earlier admission with new regard.

Bastian sighed. "But death is the cheater."

"It must have been horrible," she responded.

"Dying?"

"Feeling so hopeless."

Bastian glanced at her again, taking in the softness of her gaze, the sadness and pity that wanted to drip from her eyes. "You get used to it," he shrugged.

"Maybe you need something to live for, something that brings hope back to life…" For a second she must have forgotten what he was. She reached her small hand to touch him.

Bastian watched her slender fingers move to cover his and waited for the moment when they would sink through his surface and land on the stone like he wasn't there at all.

But they didn't move through his gossamer form.

They stopped on the surface of his own hand as though he had real, human flesh, and wasn't just a shell. He felt her warm, soft skin. He felt the dampness of slightly sweaty palms on his skin.

Bastian's wide eyes jerked toward Odette and her eyes were just as wide, her lips parted in shock.

"How?" she stuttered.

"I...I don't know. This shouldn't be possible." Bastian had not felt the touch of another human in one hundred years.

By some magic that truly only made this curse more painful, he could touch certain things; his piano, the roses in the nun's garden. He didn't fall through the seats on the trolley, or the piano bench, and he could push aside the stage curtains. When he was angry enough, he could manage to throw something small. He sometimes wished he couldn't do any of it, thinking if he had no interaction with the real world, he might have long ago drifted away into oblivion. But with all the little exceptions to his spectral existence, Bastian hadn't felt flesh and blood since the day he'd half-died. Now that he felt it, he didn't want to let go for fear it was a dream.

Bastian turned his hand under Odette's touch and curled his fingers around hers. His stomach lurched, stuck between wondering if this was a reason to hope or a game being played at his expense.

Odette squeezed his hand. "See? Hope. Something to hold on to." Her countenance brightened with the upward curving of her mouth.

For a half second, her bright eyes met his blurry gaze, and it felt like time stopped. Bastian couldn't hear any sound but her breathing. In and out; soft and steady. He swallowed down the lump gathering in his throat and opened his mouth but didn't know what to say. Should he relent or retract from this growing hope?

An older couple walked past.

Odette blinked and looked at their intertwined hands. She withdrew her fingers from his and turned toward the brook, watching the night sky.

"We should walk back." Odette tucked a fallen hair behind her ear. "I need to feed my cat."

"Of course." Bastian nodded and stepped back from the wall.

He looked down at her hand one more time and then abruptly turned and started back toward the Quarter.

They returned to the abbey courtyard in silence.

"I can accompany you the rest of the way home if you'd like?" Bastian offered.

"No, that's okay. Thank you." Odette replied with a half grin that quickly retreated. "I'm going to stop and grab a latte and sandwich from Lizzie."

"Oh, well, goodnight then." Bastian turned to go inside his dark, dilapidated fortress.

"Wait," Odette called, and he turned back. "What happened to your mother's ring? You aren't wearing it." She pointed at his empty fingers.

"I lost it." He shoved his hands back into his pockets and ignored the tear pooling at the corner of his eye.

# REFRAIN: BASTIAN 1923

Bastian twisted an imaginary band on his finger. It was missing, possibly lost or stolen. He wasn't sure which, but it was gone. It was only a phantom now, like he was only a phantom.

*It'll be done tonight.* That's what Octavian had said twelve nights ago, as Bastian was about to take the stage. If he had known it would be his last performance, he would have ended with a different song. If he had known he was about to disappear, he would have run to Catherine and begged her forgiveness.

But he didn't know.

He had bowed to the final applause and exited stage right. He had stood in the back alley for hours waiting for Octavian, waiting for some sign it would work, that it had all been worth it. As the moon had sunk, giving way to the dawn, it had occurred to Bastian that he hadn't coughed in hours. That hadn't happened in weeks. He had inhaled a long, deep breath of the new morning air and it had filled his lungs without sputtering back out in raspy heaves. He had been made whole.

Except he wasn't.

He had rushed back inside the theater looking for someone,

anyone, to share in this miracle, but it was long vacant. He had jogged through the front doors and out onto the quiet street. Only a handful of people were still meandering about; vagabonds, paperboys, late-nighters, and early risers. He had started toward his favorite diner, knowing Jack would be there early to make a fresh batch of biscuits. Making a right at the corner, he had then run right into a large man with a patched jacket.

But not into; through.

Bastian's heart and stomach had seemed to switch places. Panic coursed through his veins, making his skin tingle and his head throb. Erratic breaths pumped in and out of healed lungs. He had scanned back and forth, looking for a reaction, a face expressing equal shock. There was none to be found through his blurring vision. The man in the patched jacket had just kept walking as though nothing at all had happened to him. This wasn't possible.

Yet it was happening.

It had happened.

Twelve nights ago.

It didn't matter how many people he had tried to speak to, touch, or scream at since—no one noticed. No one flinched. They came, and they went. Police came and went. Then no one came again. Alone in the dark, Bastian crumbled, folding over into himself. His mind unraveled and tangled all at the same time as he desperately tried to make sense of it. There was no sense in it though.

Catherine was heartbroken.

Octavian was gone.

He was dead.

Except he wasn't. Was he?

Bastian sulked around the empty tables of the theater that had become his tomb. Where else could he go? He had no place of his own anymore. They had emptied his tiny flat of his possessions—of any sign that he had ever lived there—in mere hours.

His body trembled. A moan started in the back of his throat, growing into a growl, and emerging as a roar. He flung his hand, shoving a discarded champagne bottle onto the floor. Green glass splintered into a hundred fractured pieces. He stared. How was that possible? If he could connect with an object, could he still connect with the larger world? Was there hope that this was temporary, and he was coming back to himself?

Bastian repeated the move over and over until broken bits covered the floor. On his way to the stage, he knocked over chairs. He ran his fingers over the keys of the piano, a few sharp notes trickling into the air. He laughed at the minor miracle. A few days ago, he was untouchable, and the world was untouchable. He had found himself floating through it all like an invisible current.

But today…today!

Bastian tickled a familiar melody. His heart thumped in rhythm to the upbeat tempo. His foot tapped in a tiny dance.

A thud and a shatter echoed over the wooden floor.

Bastian paused mid-note and looked up to find Jimmy, the stagehand, an apple crate busted at his feet and oozing liquid. He was pointing a shaking finger at the piano. His eyes widened and his mouth gaped like a fish.

"Jimmy!" Bastian said.

The boy ignored his name.

"Jimmy, can you see me?" Bastian leaned forward, inadvertently pressing the middle C.

The boy's gaze didn't move from the piano.

"Jimmy. Jimmy!" Bastian kept repeating the name. He offered it like a prayer that would be answered if the young man would only look at him, see him, acknowledge him. "Jimmy…"

Jimmy didn't make eye contact. He only moved backward on quaking legs for three steps before turning to run away.

"No…"

Bastian pounded a fist against the keys. A march of angry chords filled the silence with the rage that poured from his heart.

There was no end to this cruel joke and no hope of return or resurrection. In a final burst, Bastian's balled fist hit the piano, resounding in a flat note that matched the pitch of his sob. Bastian sank to the ground. His fingers slid over the keys, playing a short haphazard melody before falling into his lap. A draft chilled the surrounding air. What little glow lit the space dimmed. He pulled his knees to his chest. His head hung low, and tears dripped onto his gray pants.

# CHAPTER 21

# ODETTE, 2024

Odette had not had enough caffeine that day to process what just happened.

She'd touched a ghost.

But if she could touch him, *was* he a ghost?

"Ugh," she muttered to herself as she pulled open the door to Madame Clary's—the smell of brewing coffee already reviving her brain cells.

"The usual?" Lizzie smiled, drying her hands on her apron.

"Yes. Large." Odette's stomach growled. "With a turkey club to-go."

"You got it, sweetheart," Lizzie replied. "You look like you have had quite the day."

"You have no idea." Odette offered a grateful smile and handed Lizzie a twenty from her wallet.

"You need a little break." Lizzie turned the knobs on the espresso machine. "Something fun to do, some friends to hang out with. Have you met anyone outside of me and Isabelle since moving to the city?"

Odette was tempted to spill her guts about conversations with a ghost who haunts the abandoned theater and a sassy nun who thought she had a divine mission to save him. "Not really," she muttered. "Back home, I had my sisters and church friends. I haven't been much for going out and meeting new people here just yet."

"Well, you are welcome to join me for church any Sunday you like," Lizzie said as she sprayed whipped cream on the top of Odette's latte. "We have a lot of people your age." She handed over the paper cup.

"Thank you." Odette accepted the drink and the invitation. "I just may take you up on that."

Going to church again might be just what Odette needed. She missed that community in her life and Lizzie was right. She needed some friends…real, human, alive friends.

"It's the non-denominational three blocks down," Lizzie pointed to her right. "Service starts at ten o'clock, and I'm there every week."

"Thank you," Odette replied.

"I told you; we all need people looking out for us. Joe!" She yelled over her shoulder. "You got Odette's order ready yet?"

"Coming right now!" Joe's deep reply was followed by a hand holding a brown paper bag through the pass-thru window and then a head popping behind wearing a huge grin. "And I didn't forget to add a little sweet surprise." He winked at Odette.

"Here you go, sweetie." Lizzie passed the bag to Odette.

"Thank you…again…truly." Odette took her order and turned, bumping directly into something, or rather someone. "I'm so sorry!" She quickly checked to make sure her hot coffee hadn't sloshed out of her cup and onto the stranger.

"No worries, miss," replied a man's voice with an accent that was mostly southern but layered over with something a little more foreign, maybe.

"I'm not usually this clumsy." Odette stepped back enough to get a view of the person with whom she had collided.

He was taller than her, but most people were. He was dressed like someone off the pages of *Vanity Fair* or *GQ*, with the shoulders and jawline to pull it all off. He didn't look much older than

Odette, except for the streak of gray highlighting his otherwise dark and perfectly coiffed hair.

"I am sure it was my fault entirely." He smiled, showing off white teeth and oozing charm. "I was standing much too close."

"No harm was done, so I say we're both off the hook."

"I agree." He held out his hand. "I'm Octavian, but most people prefer to call me by my last name, Zane."

"Well…Zane." She shook his hand, noting the firm grip and smooth skin. "It's nice to meet you. I'm Odette."

"The pleasure is all mine, Odette." He leaned forward, pulling her hand to his rust-colored lips to present it with a kiss, the kind you see from gentlemen in Jane Austen stories.

Odette was not one to swoon, but she was close to it, probably as close as she would ever come. "Well, I should let you order and be on my way." She stepped past him toward the door, but glanced back over her shoulder as she was stepping outside. Her cheeks heated, possibly at his smiling after her…or at Lizzie staring at her with a raised eyebrow and a smirk. Odette huffed and hustled the rest of the way outside without any further regard for either of them. Coffeehouse meet-cutes were for cheesy romance movies, and not real life.

# CHAPTER 22

# BASTIAN

Bastian stepped onto the rickety stage, the darkness of the theater thicker and more immersive than usual. There was a time when that action came with blinding lights and boisterous applause. The echo of memory swirled around him in a blur, which blackened and emptied until he remembered he was alone. He was dead…dead enough, anyway.

Just an hour ago, though, he had felt the touch of human skin for the first time in a century. Hope should be springing up inside him. Nonetheless, it was difficult to be anything other than afraid. He wanted to let his guard down. He wanted to revel in the residue of Odette's touch. He wanted to believe his curse could break.

But this one nagging thought would not let him bask in the light of hope. If he was wrong—if she could not break this curse —his despair would multiply and turn him into a monster.

A shadow swooped past Bastian. He ducked. Then he watched it circle him before coming to a stop. The reaper, wispy and dark, hovered in front of him, a tattered apparition with only hints of a form. He perceived it staring at him but saw no eyes.

"Are you here to finally finish me?" Bastian muttered. His

mouth was dry and his—what had Odette called it—his see-through heart quickened its rhythm.

The apparition didn't reply. Had it heard him? It did not acknowledge that he'd even spoken. But the air chilled his veins.

Bastian fell to his knees. "I am too weak for this life."

The reaper moved closer. A floorboard creaked behind the curtain.

"Bastian?" Sister Mary Cecilia called out from the wings.

The shadow hissed and fled.

Bastian wanted to weep. He choked down cries of confusion and weakness and exhaustion.

"Bastian, are you here?" The nun called. "Are you crying, child?" She came closer.

Bastian swallowed. "I am here," his rough words betrayed him, as he was sure they confirmed the nun's suspicion of his emotional state.

"Oh dear," she crept toward the sound of his voice. Her knees cracked as she slowly lowered herself to kneel near him. "What has happened?"

Sister Mary Cecilia's face and voice held equal amounts of compassion. It illuminated in her eyes, and Bastian wondered how this woman, who couldn't even see him, could come to show him such love. For the first time in a very long time, he wished she could see him. He wished her gaze could rest on his forlorn eyes and truly know his pain. He wished he could fall into her lap like a child looking for comfort from his mother.

"I felt her touch, Sister," Bastian replied, fighting the quiver of his lips.

"Odette's?" The nun tilted her head. "What do you mean?"

"We went for a walk. I took her to the bridge that reminds me of my mother. For a moment, she forgot. She forgot what I was, and she reached to touch me..." Bastian paused. For a brief second, he doubted it had happened. But Odette had felt it too. "She reached her hand out to mine, and I felt it...I held it."

"Oh my," Sister Mary Cecilia gasped. Her eyes blinked, and

she tilted her head thoughtfully in his direction. "That should bring joy, not despair."

"It should." Bastian agreed.

"But you are afraid," the nun stated as though she'd read his mind, because he knew she couldn't read his face.

"I want you to be right. I want Odette to be right. But I will break completely if you are both wrong."

The sister's shoulders raised and lowered as she took a deep breath. Her lips were pursed, and her eyes narrowed just a bit. She quirked her mouth to one side and seemed to be in a moment of contemplation. "Child," she finally spoke. The slow pace of her words told Bastian how measured they were. "I understand. Fear is a formidable foe."

"I want to be brave."

Sister Mary Cecilia smiled at him and shook her head. "Dearie, courage is not what defeats fear. Love does."

"Who could love me?"

"I love you. The Maker loves you. But that isn't the problem." She wiggled her finger in the air and then pointed it toward him. "You've got to accept love."

"I am not worthy of it." Bastian tasted a bitterness on his tongue with that admission.

"Real love is not earned." The nun groaned as she pushed herself off the floor one leg at a time. She rubbed her knees and then stretched her back. Her mouth opened as though she was going to say something further, but she shut it abruptly and jerked her head to the side. She reached a hand out in front of her like she was trying to touch something invisible.

Bastian wondered if she was feeling for him. But she had never done that before. "Sister?"

"Something was here. Can you feel it? The cold air here?" She leaned forward and sniffed. "Can you smell it? The hint of brimstone?"

"The reaper?" Bastian replied.

"Reaper?!" The nun laughed. "That's no reaper, at least not in the way I am sure you are thinking of it."

"Then what is it?" Bastian stood up and sniffed the air himself. He'd never considered how the thing smelled. But it was there, the sulfuric scent.

"I would guess a shadow of some sort."

"Shadow?"

"A demon, dearie." The nun said it as though it was the most normal thing in the world.

Bastian stared at her, waiting for more information or instruction. "I feel like you should be more worried."

"No, we are stronger than the darkness," she replied and smiled. "But it being here, Odette touching your hand—it means something is happening. The link between worlds—the tether keeping you in this place—it's changing."

"And you are sure that…shadow…isn't something to worry about?" Thinking the thing was a reaper coming to move his soul into eternity was one thing. Considering it a demon was different.

"Oh, shadows are nasty things, to be sure." Sister Mary Cecilia stuck out her tongue and made a noise like she tasted something unappealing. "But it can't do much if you don't let it. It only wants to feed on your despair."

"I do have plenty of that to go around," Bastian chuckled weakly.

"Listen, dearie," the nun's face hardened just a touch and her tone lowered an octave. "Do not misjudge my words. We are stronger, but that doesn't mean we don't have to fight. You cannot let that thing remain close to you."

"I didn't invite it here."

"No, you didn't. And it is probably lying in wait to see how this all plays out with your curse. It felt the shift in the veil." She paused and smiled, a gesture of reassurance. "But it is drawn to sadness and grief and pain and anger and fear, and it will suck all the good things away to keep its belly full. For a normal person, it would mean to kill them—feeding from the inside out until their body deteriorates from the destruction of their soul or they take their own life. For you, it could feed for another century, leaving you hollow in ways you haven't yet fathomed."

"What do I do?"

"Dare to hope."

Bastian closed his eyes. His shoulders dropped, and he sighed.

"I know it's hard," Sister Mary Cecilia said. "But you must try. You must focus on the good and look for the light, as I've told you before, and like I will keep telling you until you get it through your thick head. You aren't alone. I am here. The Maker is here, even if you don't believe in Him. Odette is here. She can see you. She touched you. She is trying to help you. Instead of spending so much time worrying that it won't work, consider that it will. What if it is all going to work?"

Bastian wanted to scream. He wanted to throw something, to let the tumult of emotions burst out of him. Words like hope and love—they were words from another life. Could they belong to him again? Would it be easier to let the demon feast on him until he was completely forgotten? Until even he forgot himself?

"You are worthy of His love, Bastian." The nun's voice turned soft. "As worthy as any of us." Her message was like a new song being written in his mind and heart. But it was faint—too quiet to sing along to.

He knew that Sister Mary Cecilia believed what she was saying. It sounded like truth, but it didn't feel like it. So it stayed quiet. But it was there, and Bastian didn't want to chase it away. "I will try," he whispered to the nun.

# CHAPTER 23
# ODETTE

O dette counted two hundred and thirty-seven plaster dots on the ceiling above her bed before growling and pulling her pillow over her face. She released a muffled scream and kicked her feet in a small tantrum, making Hepburn grumble and hop off the mattress.

"Sorry, sweet cat," she said, then turned over and stared at the half-closed curtains of her bedroom window.

Beyond the navy-blue fabric lay an obsidian sky full of blurry stars accented by the new moon. She remembered the tranquility of nights in her childhood backyard staring up at a similar sky. She'd welcome a little of that peace and ease right now. Her mind wouldn't shut off and allow her to sleep. No, instead of drifting into blissful shuteye, her brain had twisted and turned over thoughts of handsome men in coffee shops and breaking curses.

Odette began to think she should have just kept her head down and focused on the bookshop and binging Netflix. Talking to that nun was a mistake because now things were confusing, and she didn't like feeling confused. She didn't like emotions fluttering about, or blushing with butterflies in her stomach, or almost swooning over a stranger. She didn't like the way that touching Bastian's hand had felt in her chest.

*Bastian.* He'd started as a project. She was just going to be the Good Samaritan and help him find peace or freedom and then feel good about herself for doing it. Somewhere on the walk from the theater to the bridge, he'd become a man—a haunting, tragic man with a broken heart and shattered dreams. He'd had a mother and a father. He'd wanted things out of life. On that bridge, she'd started to see him—truly see him. When his fingers had laced with hers, she'd felt something. It was something dangerous. Bastian wasn't real in the conventional sense of the word, and she had no way of knowing that he ever would be. If they broke this curse, it could all simply mean an open door for him to pass on to the other side. There was no guarantee he would get to have a life back in full flesh and bone.

No, these feelings were murky, and she needed to tread through them carefully. Besides, maybe the goosebumps and thudding heart had been because she'd always had a thing for musicians with tragic backstories. Perhaps she simply got a little swept away in the romantic setting.

"Or maybe I am falling for ghost-boy," Odette muttered to herself.

Hepburn meowed, jumping back onto the bed, and curled against Odette's legs.

"He's not a ghost, I know," she replied to the cat. "But that doesn't mean I should just trudge forward oblivious to the facts of reality."

Hepburn meowed again.

"No, this is not about the handsome coffee-guy. He is a footnote and nothing more."

Another meow.

"Yes, he was cute. Yes, I did spend a good part of the evening wondering if I would see him again. But I don't need to be dating while in a relationship with an almost-ghost."

Hepburn looked up at her with sleepy eyes and meowed once more.

"*Working* relationship," Odette corrected her statement. She needed to talk some of this over with a person and not her cat. She also needed sleep to clear her muddled mind.

Odette turned her head to read the time on her alarm clock. It was three thirty in the morning. If she fell asleep right now, she could get six hours in and still make it to the bookshop by ten… if she didn't stop for coffee. Who was she kidding? She would have to stop for coffee. Five hours of sleep would have to be enough to get her back on track to breaking Bastian's curse and returning to a normal life. Her heart whispered a wanting. Would it be so horrible to let herself dream, if just for a moment, that a normal life included Bastian Roux? Or would it be better to keep her romantic notions focused on coffee-guy?

Odette grumbled, turned over, and covered her head with her thick comforter.

# CHAPTER 24
# OCTAVIAN

Octavian rolled up the sleeves of his pressed gray dress shirt as he stepped out onto the balcony of his hotel room. Night was always his favorite time in New Orleans. The streets buzzed with carousing and frivolity. He wouldn't go so far as to say he missed it. He would be happy to do what needed to be done and then rid himself of this city once again; to rid himself of Bastian and all that reminded him of the hollow man.

He wrapped his fingers around the cool cast-iron railing and squeezed. His knuckles twinged. He cursed under his breath.

Age was catching up to him. He felt it in the sudden ache of his bones. He saw it in the way his skin subtly wrinkled over his hands. They were perfectly young and smooth just hours ago.

He growled.

That girl—Odette—was part of it. Octavian didn't know her exact role in this century-old play, but it couldn't be a coincidence that the curse began to weaken when she'd arrived in Bastian's vicinity. He didn't trust that kind of serendipity. Juleanne could have created her curse with some loophole—a thread this Odette was somehow pulling. While Meg continued to look for the key so he could lock this curse tight for eternity, he would keep an eye on Odette—a close eye.

to look for the key so he could lock this curse tight for eternity, he would keep an eye on Odette—a close eye.

# CHAPTER 25

# ODETTE

Odette smoothed the wrinkles of her floral skirt before stepping inside the double glass doors of Lizzie's church. A cheery older fellow in a navy-blue sport coat said hello and shook her hand, then pointed her toward the lobby. Little groups of parishioners chatted around brown leather couches and cafe tables. Odette squeezed the strap of her purse as if it was a lifeline. A Saturday night spent binge-watching had left her with the notion that her soul needed more rest than Netflix could offer. While she had sipped her morning coffee, she'd remembered Lizzie's invitation to church and thought it was just the ticket. She forgot how awkward it could be—being new in a foyer filled with people who were already friends. She was the odd woman out and fought the urge to run away.

"Odette!" A smooth, warm southern accent bounced through the space.

She turned to see Lizzie waving at her and holding a coffee pot.

"Come here, girl. Can I pour you a cup?" She didn't wait for an answer though and was already pouring steaming coffee into a paper cup.

"Don't you get enough of pouring coffee for people during the week?" Odette laughed as she took the welcome gift.

"What can I say? I love serving people. Hospitality is in my spirit."

"That it is," Odette smiled.

"I'm glad to see you this morning," Lizzie started before music coming from the sanctuary doors interrupted her. "Service is starting. You can sit with me if you'd like."

"I would, thank you." Odette followed Lizzie into the auditorium. The woman waved at a few people and walked like she knew exactly where she was going in the maze of seats.

The two of them tucked into a row where Lizzie's husband Joe was already sitting. Lizzie poked his shoulder and he stood. They both started to sing a song that was somewhat familiar to Odette. A lot of this church was familiar to her. Faces were different, but the feeling was like coming home. She let the presence melt through her layers of confusion and anxiety, bringing with it a peace she hadn't felt in longer than she'd realized. The recognition of something her soul had been longing for penetrated her skin and made her heart thump harder against her chest. She opened her mouth to sing, and tears accompanied her quiet melody.

Lizzie handed her a tissue which she gratefully accepted.

"Come with me," the woman whispered, gently taking Odette's hand, leading her back out to the foyer.

"I'm sorry," Odette said as the auditorium doors closed behind them.

"Girl, don't be sorry for feeling." She led Odette to a pair of leather chairs in the corner of the lobby. "You just looked like you needed a breath and maybe a friend."

Odette dabbed the already damp tissue under her misty eyes. "I don't know what came over me in there."

"Jesus," Lizzie chuckled and patted her knee. "He has a way of getting through our masks and pretenses and pointing right to the heart of a burden we are carrying."

"Burden feels like the right word and the wrong one."

"I understand that." Lizzie pressed a hand to her tight black curls, primping her hair a touch as she sat back in the seat.

Odette waited for her to ask a question or push the conversation further, but she didn't. She sat silent, her bright yellow tassel earrings dangling next to her brown skin while her eyes looked off into the space in front of them.

Odette took a sip of the coffee that she'd almost forgotten she was holding. "Sometimes a burden doesn't feel like one, and sometimes something that isn't a burden does feel like one. It's hard to tell why or what makes a thing turn heavy," Odette whispered, not sure why she was even saying this out loud.

"In my experience, things get heavy when we are carrying them wrong," Lizzie replied. She turned her gaze back toward Odette and raised an eyebrow. "Are you carrying something wrong?"

"I have no clue," Odette laughed. "Chances are good since I'm not even sure it's something I'm supposed to carry…I mean, I think I am because I'm the only one who…" Odette stopped herself before she said something that made her sound crazy. "I'm trying to help a friend."

"Ah," Lizzie nodded. "That can get complicated. We don't always know which part we are supposed to carry, and which part is solely theirs."

"Complicated is the right word for it. Complicated and confusing."

Lizzie leaned forward, her head tilted in curiosity, and a smile nudged the corners of her lips upward. "Are we talking about a man?"

"No…" Does a ghost-boy count? "Well, yes. But it's not what you think." Odette's cheeks warmed and she took another sip of coffee to give herself a moment to compose.

"You don't have to tell me the sordid details…unless you want to," Lizzie winked. "I know what it's like to have feelings get muddy and you can't see clearly."

"What do you do?"

"You pray. You slow down. You focus on what is clear," Lizzie replied.

"He...my friend...needs help. That much is clear."

"And you can help him?"

"I think so. I hope so." She was likely the only one who could help him. Maybe she was even meant to help him.

"Then focus on what you can do for him, what is in the realm of your ability. Leave the rest to the Lord. It won't get rid of all the mud, but it might keep you from sinking in it." Lizzie sat up. "After all, we are no one's Messiah. I don't know what your friend is going through, but I know *we* can't do the saving. We usually just hold a person's hand and lead them to the One who does. The rest is up to them." She held out her hand to Odette.

Odette took it and squeezed. "Thank you."

"Anytime, darlin'." Lizzie stood up and pulled Odette with her. "Now, how about we go back in there and listen to what the pastor has to say this mornin'?"

"Yes, ma'am."

"Don't be calling me ma'am now. I'm not that old." Her rich laugh punctuated the wisdom she had given Odette, sealing the moment with joy.

## CHAPTER 26
# ODETTE

Raindrops pelted against the glass windows of the bookstore, creating a percussive soundtrack to Odette's studying. She loved rainy days—the gray sky and the soothing ambiance. Isabelle had brought her a cup of tea that steamed beside her while she read through her pile of books. She'd pulled six volumes from the shelves in the shop. The other eleven were courtesy of the local library. Pouring through books, while a little more time-consuming, was more productive than Google searches—at least on this topic. Odette liked books better anyway. Perhaps going from jumbled and confusing letters to having the tools and ability to decipher words in a way that matched her brain had given her a sense of power. The smell and the feel of soft pages between her fingers conjured a certain kind of magic. A kid who'd hated reading and now adored it.

It was also quite satisfying to slam a book closed when no answers were uncovered and her frustration started to build. Which it did, and she did—four times. She'd thought she was on to something a few days ago when she found the list of practitioners. But unless Bastian could pull a memory he didn't have from the recesses of his mind, she didn't know where to go with that. She needed a recipe for a curse—for Bastian's curse.

"Ugh," Odette grumbled under her breath. When had her life gotten so weird?

She took a sip of her tea and then stuffed a cookie into her mouth. She took another book from her stack and flipped through its pages. This was a collection of photos and paintings dating back to the 1800s. Some were of places, others were repre-sentations of events or rituals. Many were portraits. As Odette glanced through the images, a few names popped from the captions and grabbed her attention. She realized that she recog-nized them and searched through the stack for the book she had brought to Bastian earlier. The lineage she'd discovered gave her hope that they could find the queen who'd created and was capable of breaking Bastian's curse. She scanned the list and matched names to black-and-white faded faces. Bastian didn't know a name, but perhaps he would recognize a face. It was worth a shot.

The bell on the front door jingled.

Odette turned her book over and got up to help the incoming customer.

"Good afternoon," she said.

"So we meet again," coffee-guy replied. He was as dapper as he had been when she'd bumped into him at Madame Clary's even as he brushed water droplets from the shoulders of his suit jacket. "Odette, wasn't it?"

"Yes, Octavian Zane." He smiled when she remembered his name and her insides tumbled. The way he looked at her made her cheeks flush warm and she hoped not too red. "Can I help you find a book?"

"I'm not looking for anything in particular. In my travels, I like to peruse shops in search of antique tomes and first editions to add to my collection." He ran his fingers over the spines that lined the shelf next to where he stood.

"There are treasures to be found in the used book section toward the back, but we have some rare jewels here." Odette pulled her key to unlock the glass case next to the front counter.

"Assuming you could talk Isabelle into parting with any of them."

"I can be very persuasive." He grinned and bit his bottom lip before turning his attention to the now-accessible books.

Odette silently reminded herself not to swoon and ignored the weak feeling in her knees. Why was she such a sucker for a charming accent?

"I see you're interested in my collection." Isabelle, who had been lingering nearby, stepped up to the pair. "Is there a particular book you're searching for?"

Octavian's mouth curled into his charming smile that suddenly looked to Odette to be a mix between the handsome prince and devilish villain. "Nothing specific," he replied. "I am drawn to the particularly rare." He glanced at Odette.

Isabelle followed his gaze, raising a brow at Odette. The old woman seemed to stifle a silent giggle before turning her attention back to the customer and the books. "I have an illustrated edition of Peter Pan in Kensington Gardens, some early Hans Christian Andersen, and my favorite is a first edition of *La Belle et la Bête...*"

"*Beauty and the Beast*," Octavian responded. "So you have a fancy for fairytales?" He seemed less than impressed by the selection.

"Oh, I have what some might call more serious works as well..." Isabelle was undeterred. "But make no mistake, fairytales are not just for children. They are stories that remind us what it is to fear and dream and believe in something more. They are peeks into the soul. For instance, G. K. Chesterton wrote of this tale, 'There is the great lesson of *Beauty and the Beast*, that a thing must be loved before it is lovable.'"

"Love is overrated," Octavian replied, "and in my opinion, so are fairytales." He caught Odette's eye. His mouth tightened briefly, then he laughed, as though the whole statement might have been a joke.

"Perhaps you have only known cheap love," Isabelle countered, then shut the glass case and locked it.

Odette was a bit shocked at Isabelle's curt response. Maybe because she had been wrestling with her own opinions on love recently and was no longer quite sure where she stood on the matter. She had grown up on fairytales, at least the Disney versions. Once upon a time, she'd believed in true love, but she didn't think she still did now. Or did she? Was the hope of a rich love still lingering in the shadows of her heart? She hadn't flinched at Octavian's cynicism, but she didn't fully hold it either. Had he read something in her eyes that had caused him to soften his remark with that forced chuckle? Was she softening to love again? No. She mentally shut herself down. That kind of thinking was dangerous. Especially when the source might be a century-old half-dead man only she could see.

"Someone has taken an interest in voodoo," Octavian interrupted her internal interrogation. He had turned toward her study table and the stack of books thereupon.

"Odette has found a hobby," Isabelle answered with a cool stare directed toward coffee-guy.

"Seems a strange interest for such a lively young woman." Octavian opened and closed the cover of one book and tapped a finger on her notepad.

Odette quickly grabbed the legal pad and flipped it over to conceal her scribbles. "When in New Orleans?" she shrugged and smiled. It was uneasy. The whole moment had turned awkward, and not just because of her normal level of personal awkwardness. The charming gentleman had darkened somehow. Was it the look in his eyes or the clench of his jaw? Had there been a shift in his tone that was setting off warning lights in her mind? Was it Isabelle's guarded attitude toward him? Whatever it was, any butterflies that had once swarmed in her stomach had now disappeared completely.

"This city will do that to you," he replied, then looked at his watch. "I must be going, but it was nice to see you again, Odette." He dipped his head in a cordial bow.

Odette returned the gesture and held her breath as she watched him leave. When he was gone without another word, she exhaled.

"He's handsome, that's for sure." Isabelle frowned. "But I don't like him."

"I don't think I do either," Odette replied.

# CHAPTER 27

# ODETTE

Odette's legs dangled from the edge of the dusty stage. A camping lantern sat beside her, illuminating about a ten-foot circumference of Bastian's theater, her books, and three cartons of takeout. She used chopsticks to shovel chicken and broccoli into her mouth while she flipped the pages of the book on her lap.

"I see you have made yourself quite at home." Bastian's voice wafted from somewhere behind her. Piano keys tinkled a brief melody.

"If I'm going to do all this research to help you, the least you can allow is my dinner picnic." Odette switched out cartons for the fried rice. She took a bite and spoke through her full mouth. "Besides, we are never going to get anywhere if I can't eat and work at the same time."

"Have we gotten somewhere?" Bastian asked, coming to sit beside her. His face scrunched a bit in concentration.

She hadn't noticed before how aberrant it was, Bastian's connection to the world around him. The surreal and nonsensical nature, the lack of logic in the ways he was able or unable to interact with the tangible and solid. What must it be like to be present in reality and yet also somehow not?

Bastian cleared his throat. "Did you hear my question? Because ignoring a man who can't be sure if he has faded back into total oblivion is rather rude."

"Sorry, ghost-boy." Odette set down her carton of food and picked up her book.

"Not a ghost," Bastian muttered under his breath.

"This stack isn't even half of the books I've been perusing the last couple of days, but while there's so much you can find about voodoo, it's all pretty surface-level stuff. The real is secret. I'm beginning to think I won't find our answer in a book."

Bastian exhaled a slow breath. "Answers may not be found at all."

"Don't give up on me yet." Odette flipped pages. "Remember when I showed you the names of voodoo queens?"

Bastian nodded.

"Well, you didn't recognize any of the names, but maybe you will recognize a face." She tilted the book so he could see the printed images.

"I told you, I didn't go near any of that...."

"That doesn't mean they didn't come near to you," Odette interrupted. "Just look. It can't hurt to look."

She slowly flipped the pages, allowing Bastian time to consider the likenesses and to search for them in his memories. Page after page, he merely shook his head and furrowed his brow. His shoulders drooped, and Odette wondered if he was losing faith with each photo that offered no recognition.

But then his eyes suddenly widened. He pointed a translucent finger. "Stop! There! That!"

"You know her?" Odette read the caption, "Madame Juleanne..."

"No," Bastian replied. "I don't know her, but I know that— the ring she's wearing on her necklace." He leaned forward and squinted his eyes for a better look. "I believe it was mine."

Odette yanked the book away from him and examined it for herself. The image was faded with time and the ring was so small. She pulled out her smartphone and used the camera to zoom in on the tiny piece of the photo. It was fuzzy, but you could make out what appeared to be a rose etched into the metal. "Your grandfather's ring?"

"Yes," Bastian replied.

"How can you be sure? It's not exactly easy to see the details."

"That ring was the one treasure I owned—my dearest possession. I rarely took it off, then one day it was just gone. But that is it." Bastian stood and began to pace. "How would this woman have gotten it? Could it have been her who did this to me?"

Odette tried to focus in on what he was saying. "So your grandfather's ring goes missing right about the time you are cursed to live as a ghost and you didn't put the pieces together?" Odette raised an eyebrow. It was likely an unfair question, but she had a sudden nagging suspicion that Bastian wasn't telling her everything.

"Sorry." Bastian rolled his eyes. "I was going through some things that month, and losing my grandfather's ring just wasn't at the top of my priority list, what with the cursing and the dying and the heartbreaking..."

"Don't get sassy with me, ghost-boy," Odette retorted. "You've had a hundred years to investigate the details. I just thought perhaps you'd have had a little time to add some things up."

"Not a ghost, and perhaps I could have been a little more proactive, but despair is a formidable foe. Besides, it's not like I can waltz into the local library and check out a book." Bastian retreated to his piano bench.

Odette stood and followed him. "You could have. The nun would have helped..."

"The nun helps enough. Between the two of you, all the help and sarcasm may be the thing that is my final undoing." He played a few solemn notes. "Besides, I never really considered I could be helped. What good would it have done to sort out the details if they couldn't save me?"

Odette slid onto the bench beside him and placed her hand on his. The sensation tingled through her fingers like static. "I'm sorry."

"Don't be." Bastion turned his hand over beneath hers until they were palm to palm. He held it for a second before withdrawing his hands to his lap. "I didn't have hope until you...It kind of terrifies me."

"You think you're scared? I'm the one talking to a ghost." Odette bumped against him and laughed.

"Not a ghost," Bastian replied, one corner of his mouth drawing upward into the slightest smile. "I want to show you something."

# CHAPTER 28

# ODETTE

Bastian swung his feet around the piano bench to face the opposite direction. He seemed suddenly resolute but rephrased his question, "May I show you something?"

"Okay," Odette said. Her curiosity was even more piqued by the shy downturn of Bastian's gaze. "Lead the way."

With a timid shake of his head, Bastian stood. "We'll need to take the streetcar."

Odette followed him out of the theater and to the street, where they only had to wait three minutes for the next trolley to arrive. They boarded and Bastian gestured for Odette to take a seat. She was about to move over to give him room to sit beside her.

"I'll stand," he said. "I think it will be less awkward given how full these can get this time of day.

No sooner had he spoken the words than a mother with two elementary-age children got on and walked right through Bastian. He winced and Odette wondered if it hurt him when that happened.

"It doesn't hurt," he said, likely reading her question from her furrowed brow. "It's like when your foot falls asleep and then wakes up."

Odette nodded. She was careful not to reply out loud or stare too intently at the invisible man next to her.

"You get used to it after a while." Bastian shrugged. He looked around, perusing the other public transportation patrons. An older gentleman was reading just across the aisle. A middle-aged woman sat with headphones on, her eyes closed. Two teenagers toward the back were laughing at their smartphone screens. The bell dinged. The trolley stopped and the two boys exited, causing another wince from Bastian as they walked past.

One said to the other, "He's got no rizz."

"No cap," was the reply then another round of laughter.

"Now that I will never get used to." Bastian wrinkled his nose. "What are those words even supposed to mean? How is someone supposed to keep up with a century's worth of changing lingo."

Odette stifled a giggle.

"I'll have to add those words to my list." Bastian now talked more to himself than Odette, which only made her want to laugh more, but she maintained her composure until the trolley stopped again.

"This is our stop," Bastian said.

When they were out of earshot, Odette finally released the laughter she'd been holding in. "You have a running list of words you don't understand?"

"As a matter of fact, I do."

"Is it written down somewhere or just in your head? Because I would love to see it." She continued to snicker as Bastian led her down a residential street. "What's on it? Tubular? Fleek? Triflin'?" While Bastian looked less than amused—to the point that she knew at least one of her guesses was certainly on his list —she couldn't help herself. It was somewhat adorable that her grouchy ghost-boy was miffed at modern slang, of all things.

"If you are finished, we are here." Bastian stopped in front of a small brick house with a covered front porch and a cobblestone sidewalk leading to a yellow front door.

At first glance, it was an adorable cottage. But upon closer inspection, the ravages of time and neglect were glaring. The grass was in desperate need of cutting. Weeds poked through the walkway and the bushes framing the front steps were vastly overgrown. The porch stairs and floor were rickety and creaked with each step Odette took toward the front door, whose paint was chipped and peeling.

"Would you open the door?" Bastian waited to the left.

"Are you sure we should?"

"No one has lived in this house for at least five years. It will be fine. I promise."

Odette turned the brass knob. At first, it seemed locked but then it clicked and the door nudged open. As she crossed the threshold, the smell of mothballs and mildew invaded her nostrils. She sneezed.

"It used to be neat as a pin…always perfectly kept," Bastian said as he stopped to stand in the middle of the empty room.

The wood floors were scratched, and cobwebs hung from ceiling corners, but there was a character and charm to the vintage woodwork and fixtures.

"And it always smelled like Catherine's perfume and her mother's home cooking." Bastian inhaled like he was reaching for a memory.

"Catherine lived here?" Odette took ginger steps closer to him.

He glanced toward her with a sad smile. "Yes," his reply fumbled out. "Until the day she died." He paused then took a deep breath. "I used to spend every Sunday evening here with her. After church, her mother would cook the best food you'd have ever eaten. Then we'd listen to the radio and dance right here in front of the window. I'd give her a spin and she'd laugh, and it was the best music I'd ever heard."

"She sounds lovely," Odette said, sensing a warmth she hadn't yet seen in Bastian. Watching and listening to him relive joyous memories was like perceiving new parts of him.

"She was," he said. "She would come to the theater every weekend to watch me play. In that crowded room, her face was the only one that mattered, like a pin light was pointing right at her and everyone else faded into the dark." Bastian looked at the ground. The room chilled. He pointed at a spot just a few feet in front of him. "That's where she sat when I broke her heart. She cried so hard she could barely breathe, and leaving her like that shattered something in me. I didn't deserve her."

*Is this why he thinks he doesn't deserve help?* Odette almost asked him the question but the look on his face was all the answer she needed. "She was part of your deal with the devil."

"I don't know why," he muttered. "Was she an ingredient to this curse or was it just spite and envy…it doesn't matter." He stood very still for a moment, just staring at that spot. Then he looked to another space in the room, and then another, like he was following the ghost of her memory. "I came here after I realized…what I'd become. She stood right here when they told her I'd disappeared and they thought I was dead. I watched her heart break all over again as she fell to the floor sobbing. But the thing about living outside of time is you get to watch it pass. While it was passing me by, it carried her forward. I saw her heart crack and then I saw it heal, and I was glad for that small mercy."

"You kept coming back here?"

Bastian glanced at Odette and shook his head. "Oh, yes. Often at first, then less and less as time went on, but I kept coming back here. I figured I could be a witness to her life if not a participant." Bastian walked toward a discolored spot on the wall over the fireplace where a picture or painting must have once hung. "She fell in love again and got married. She lost her mother, but her husband would hold her while she grieved. She had babies—two boys and a girl that looked just like her. While I stayed forever young, she watched her children graduate and have children of their own before she died holding her husband's hand."

Odette wiped her wet face as he talked. She wanted to hug him, to hold him and relieve some of the sorrow that seemed to make his shoulders slump under its weight. She stepped toward him, reaching for his hand, when he suddenly spun toward her, startling her to a stop.

"I think she saw me," he blurted. "When she passed from this life, I stood at the end of the bed, and I would swear she looked right at me and smiled."

"I bet she did," Odette bit her quivering lip.

"I was a witness to her life." A tear escaped the corner of his eye and dripped down his cheek and hovered on his chin before he wiped it off and turned back to the wall.

"Why would you put yourself through all that? It had to hurt."

"It did," he replied. "Some days it felt like I was only torturing myself—which I probably deserved—but some days it was just beautiful."

"You didn't deserve the torture." Odette did take his hand this time, tugging it and his attention. "I think Catherine would agree with me."

"Oh, she most definitely would have. You both share a certain spunk and tenacious optimism." He chuckled. "You know, I think I brought you here so you could understand my despair and scare you away by my monstrous actions of the past, but..."

"It didn't work." She shrugged. "I saw past it right to your warm, gooey center, and now you will never be rid of me."

Odette smiled a big cheesy grin to break the tension. Without really thinking she mingled her fingers with Bastian's and when he squeezed them, she scolded herself. This daydream was getting a bit treacherous. Her reckless heart might be the next one broken.

# CHAPTER 29
# BASTIAN

Bastian sat at his piano that evening, occasionally raising his fingers to play a note, but every time, he ended up dropping them back to his lap before they could make contact with the ivory keys. Music was his solace, but the more time and energy focused on breaking this curse—the more time with Odette—the further from peace he moved. Shouldn't it be the opposite? Had he learned to find comfort in his melancholy half-existence?

Their trip to Catherine's house had left him raw and confused. The story he'd told himself over and over again was that he was to be despised, but remembering Catherine's deathbed smile, and the way Odette had looked at him in the empty living room, those things didn't fit that narrative. He was imperfect and had made a selfish decision because he was terrified of death but…could he still be loved?

Floorboards creaked.

Bastian looked up and across the stage, waiting to see who would come into view. Odette had left just half an hour before. Was Sister Mary Cecilia coming to bring him more flowers and encouragement? The figure emerging from the shadow into the light of Odette's forgotten lantern belonged to neither woman. This silhouette was tall and lean.

"What? No jazz melody to get the audience on their feet?" He recognized the slithering, smooth voice before the face came into view. "Oh wait, I guess there hasn't been an audience in quite some time." Octavian smirked.

Bastian jumped to his feet, his bench wobbling but not falling over. He clenched his fists, ready to strike this unwelcome visitor, tear away his arrogant air. "Zane, why are you here?" A growl rumbled in Bastian's throat. Octavian's mischievous eyes stared straight into his, giving him pause. "Wait. You can see me?"

"I guess that's my curse," Octavian shrugged. His upper lip curled in disgust. "Trust me, I'd rather not."

For a moment, through Octavian's contempt, Bastian's rage mingled with relief as he made the connection. He knew Octavian had set all this into motion. He was connected to this curse and could see Bastian. If Odette could also see him, it meant she was somehow connected to it, too. She and the nun had been right. There was a reason.

If Bastian wasn't staring into the face of his personal devil, he would have played a song, a number the imaginary audience could dance to.

All the joy retreated as quickly as it had come and suspicion took its place. He repeated, "Why are you here?"

"I think you know why," Octavian replied. "Something has shifted. Something is happening. Something, or some*one*, is messing around with my hard work."

Odette.

"See there." Octavian pointed at him. "I can see it on your face, in your eyes. You have something to lose again." He took five steps forward and placed his hands on the top of Bastian's piano. "It's that girl, isn't it?"

"I'm sure I don't know what you are talking about," Bastian lied.

Octavian let out a deep laugh. "You never had a good poker face, my friend. I've seen her come in and out of this theater. Odette." There was both bite and music in the way he said her name—sharp notes, slightly softened by his blended accent.

"She can't do anything." Bastian slumped onto his bench. His fingers tickled the dusty keys, releasing a few half-hearted notes into the air but leaving no prints. "She is out of her depth."

"I hope you are right..." Octavian leaned forward. The glow of the lantern's light cast shadows over his face, darkening his features. But it also illuminated the gray streak in his hair.

Bastian squinted at it. A few decades ago, he had caught a glimpse of Octavian hustling down an avenue here in the Quarter. It was a glance from across the street, and he was sure Zane hadn't noticed him, but Bastian had paid attention. This was his friend-turned-enemy popping into his city at a time when Bastian had still dreamed of freedom and revenge. There was no gray in his hair then, no wrinkles around his eyes. Octavian had looked exactly the same as he had the last day they'd spoken in the back alley. Were these new signs of age natural though unnaturally slow, or were they something else? Something might truly be shifting in Bastian's favor.

There was a time when Bastian thought Octavian was nothing more than a pal down on his luck. He was just a guy always looking for a good deal or big break—at worst, he might have been a harmless charlatan. Not now. Now he saw the villain behind the charming demeanor; the devil wearing a tailored suit. He couldn't take anything else from Bastian, but...

"You won't hurt her," Bastian ordered.

Octavian chuckled. "What will stop me? You?" Octavian stood straight again and adjusted the cuffs of his jacket. "What I will or won't do depends on you, friend." A sneer punctuated his drawled, icy words. Octavian turned to leave. "But I will certainly not let her undo me," he said as he left.

A month ago, Bastian would have ripped apart the pieces of the stage he could touch, leaving chaos in the wake of his frustration. He would have cursed the void which kept him from revenge. There was a part of him that wanted to do just that right now, but it was a feeling that was shrinking—tempered somehow. He stayed at the piano, drumming the keys and trying to decipher if the reason was hope or fear. A chill ran over Bastian's neck and arms. His companion shadow, the reaper, drifted over the stage.

# CHAPTER 30
# ODETTE

Odette stepped out of the sun lighting the sidewalk and into the shadows of the narrow alleyway. Her mother's voice whispered in her head that this wasn't the type of place she should be, that she should turn around and go back to her apartment and leave crooked things alone. But the tingle she still felt across her palm pushed her forward, ignoring her internal warnings. She hadn't been able to shake the sensation of Bastian's hand touching hers, and she didn't want to. She wanted to feel it again. More terrifying than the shop behind the black door at the end of the alley was the notion that she never would get to touch him again.

"Pull yourself together, Odette," she muttered under her breath as her legs wobbled with each step. It's an herbalist shop now, anyway—no voodoo. And you're just here to ask questions.

The frosted glass of the door read *Barbot's Tinctures and Tonics*, in a fancy font that swirled and curled. Odette turned the cold brass knob and pushed. The door squeaked across the wood floor, sticking enough to require a little extra effort on her part before stepping inside.

"I'm so sorry about that door," a friendly voice said. "I keep meaning to fix it and every time I set my mind to do it, something distracts me." Behind the counter was a young black woman with hair tucked under a brightly colored scarf, gold hoops dangling from her ears, and a huge grin warming her face.

"It's no worries," Odette replied.

"What can I help you with today?"

Odette couldn't help but return the woman's comforting smile. "I'm looking for information on Juleanne Barbot." Odette pulled a folded photocopy from her purse—the black-and-white image of Juleanne wearing Bastian's ring—and handed it to the woman.

The shopkeeper lost her smile. As her face cooled, so did the atmosphere, bringing goosebumps to the surface of Odette's arms.

"I found this picture of her," Odette said in the cheeriest voice she could offer without seeming insane. "I'm looking for this ring."

The shopkeeper stared at the image with wide eyes but refused to touch the paper. She just squinted at the ring like it was the most terrifying thing she'd ever seen.

"I'm Odette, by the way." She held out her free hand.

"I'm Meg." The shopkeeper's fingers quivered as she completed the handshake. "And I don't mean to be rude, but whatever you are looking for is best left lost."

"I don't think that it is." Odette was too close to quit now. Even if the warning in Meg's words made her stomach twist into a tight knot. "Not when it's for a friend."

"Mama?" A little boy stepped from the back room with a juice box in his hands and a familiarity with Meg written in his features.

Meg opened the juice and handed it back to him. "You go on back in the office, baby." She returned her attention to Odette and sighed. "Look, I don't know you and you don't know me, but there's someone else looking for that ring and..."

"Someone else?"

"Someone you don't want to cross." Meg rubbed her wrists. "You've gotten yourself mixed up in something dangerous."

"I know this is about a curse," Odette said. She'd be lying if she hadn't thought there was darkness at play; cruelty, and perhaps evil. But Bastian was none of those things. He deserved her bravery now. "But my friend…"

"Yes, your friend is cursed. And someone did that to him and they aren't just going to let you undo it." Meg bit out the words in a scolding whisper.

"Who?"

Meg glanced warily around the room, then leaned a little closer to Odette. "It's bad enough you're here and we are having this conversation. Bad for you *and* bad for me and…my family." She looked back toward where the boy had gone. A tear dripped down her cheek and she erased it with a quick swipe. "Don't ask me questions that'll only make it worse."

Odette couldn't speak. Only nod. She looked back at the black-and-white photo still in her hand. "Is there a question I can ask?"

Meg glanced at the picture. "Not today…but…leave that with me."

Odette fought the urge to smile and handed over the photocopy.

Meg quickly folded it up and shoved it into the pocket of her jeans. "I want to help you…much better you than him…but we need to be careful. He's watching you."

A cold sensation washed over Odette and her knotted stomach tumbled and dropped. If Bastian wasn't the villain of this story, someone else had to be. That she knew. But it had never occurred to her that they would be here now. "How? Why?" The tiny questions spilled out of her quivering lips.

Meg's hand grabbed Odette's and gave it a quick squeeze. "He and Bastian are linked. One stays half-dead so the other can stay fully alive. That's the nature of this curse, but something shifted…it's weakening."

Odette blinked. All the riddled pieces were coming together. Bastian was an easy target for someone else's gain. But it was unraveling now.

"Because of me?" Another unintentional question fumbled into the open. The nun had said that her being able to see him mattered. Is this why? But how could she be wrapped up in a one-hundred-year-old curse? She hadn't even been alive when it was cast.

"I don't know," Meg said. "Maybe." Her eyes darted around the shop, toward the back office, the doorway, and the windows again. She let go of Odette's hand and took a step back. "But we can't keep talking about it—not here." Her eyes shut tight, and her chin trembled. "Please."

"Are you sure you want to help me?" Odette whispered. This woman seemed so scared. She had a child. Could Odette ask this of her?

Meg inhaled a deep breath. "If he is stopped, we are all safer."

"Then where? When?" Odette whispered.

"I don't know that either." She wrung her hands. "But I'll figure something out."

"Thank you," Odette said, the tiniest bit of relief lifting her heavy shoulders. She was closer to answers and closer to Bastian's freedom, even if that also meant she was also closer to danger herself.

# CHAPTER 31
# ODETTE

Odette glanced over her shoulder about every fifth step that she took from Meg's shop to Lizzie's cafe. No one lurked in shadows or ducked behind lamp-posts. But Meg had gotten under her skin, which now tingled and twitched as though eyes were certainly watching her. She told herself it didn't matter. The danger had always been there. The fact that she now knew about it served only to keep her alert.

A car horn beeped and Odette startled.

Inhaling a deep breath, she pushed her glasses up her nose. She would not be ridiculous and jittery. She simply would not. Her sweaty palms turned the knob on the cafe entrance.

"Hey there, darlin'," Lizzie welcomed her with a wide grin. "Your usual?"

Odette approached the counter. "Let's go with decaf this time."

Lizzie tilted her head and arched one brow. "Everything okay?"

"Yeah," Odette squeaked. "Just trying to balance my caffeine intake in the evenings. It's a test run. We'll see how it goes."

"Whatever you say." Lizzie looked less than convinced, but

turned her attention to the espresso machine and went to work. "Anything to eat?"

"No, thanks."

"Here ya go then." Lizzie handed off the steaming cup.

"Thank you." Odette traded the cup for a five-dollar bill and grabbed a lid from the stack on the counter.

"Woah, there." An eccentric accent interrupted her turn to exit.

"Sorry." Odette looked up to find Octavian Zane just three inches away from her.

"We've got to stop running into each other like this," he said, lips curling into a charming smile.

She tucked a loose hair behind her ear. "That we do."

"Would you like to sit and enjoy that latte with some conversation?" he asked, and something indiscernible flashed across his eyes.

"I'm…I'm sorry, but I can't this evening. I already have plans with a friend."

"That's too bad," Zane replied. "Perhaps another time?"

"Sure." Odette regretted the response the moment it left her lips. While he was certainly handsome in a swoony, Hollywood way, she couldn't shake how she'd felt after their bookstore conversation.

Even more red flags were waving as she stepped past him to leave. She shook them away and turned toward the theater. Flirty coffee shop guys were not on her list of things to spend emotional energy on this evening.

Gentle humming floated from inside the iron fence of the abbey courtyard. Sister Mary Cecilia was accompanying her rose-tending with a soft tune. Yesterday the red flowers had been in full bloom, now they were withered around the edges.

"The flowers look a little droopy today," Odette said.

"Yes," the sister replied. "I came out this morning and they had seemed to wilt." She spritzed them with a purple glass mister. "They aren't the only ones."

"Bastian?"

"He is fragile today, dearie." Sister Mary Cecilia reached into her pocket and handed Odette the key.

"What happened?"

"His past returned."

Odette nodded, taking the key but not understanding what the nun meant. Bastian's past was long dead—most of it, anyway.

She hurried to unlock the theater door. Her feet knew the way to the stage, and she was calling his name before reaching the curtains.

"Bastian?"

She flipped the switch on the camping lantern she had left behind and a soft glow pushed back the dark.

"Bastian? Ghost-boy?"

"Not a ghost."

His voice was a rough whisper, but its sound offered her a small consolation. She did her best to hold on to that morsel of comfort as he walked to the edge of the stage with slumped shoulders and tired eyes. He ran translucent fingers through his gossamer curls.

"Are you okay?" Odette sat next to him.

"I am fine, Odette."

"You're lying."

Bastian didn't give any sign that he was going to respond to her accusation.

"I think I have someone willing to help us," Odette began to explain about Meg and her grandmother. "Maybe your ring is the key to the whole thing…"

"I need you to stop," Bastian said, staring at the floor.

"Excuse me?"

"I need you to please stop. Stop researching. Stop looking. Stop trying to help me." His voice raised a notch with each word as his eyes barely glanced in her direction.

Feelings of anger and compassion that Odette didn't even

know could occupy the same space coursed out from her thumping heart all the way to her tingling fingers and toes. Her cheeks warmed and her armpits were sweaty.

"No." She exhaled the word, staring right at him, waiting for him to look at her.

His jaw clenched. "Odette...please."

*Please.* The word was pleading and desperate. This wasn't his normal pessimism at work, but whatever it was it didn't change her own mind.

"No, " Odette said. This time the single word was a decimal louder and an octave deeper.

"Things have changed. It's dangerous for you to..."

Her compassion inched closer to frustration. She huffed. "I don't need to be protected like I'm some lost kitten. I'm a big girl, Bastian. I can..."

"He came here, Odette. He threatened you." Bastian looked at her now, with terror clouding his blue eyes.

"Who?" A chill flitted over her arms, leaving a trail of goosebumps.

"The perpetrator of my curse." Bastian swallowed. "Octavian Zane."

Odette gasped. She couldn't remember ever having actually gasped in her life before. Not even at scary movies. But at the mention of that name, she'd audibly gasped—hand to her mouth and everything. All those meet-cutes weren't flukes. "He's been watching me."

"What?"

Odette chastised herself for saying those last words out loud. "Zane. I've met him. A couple of times now."

"He's spoken to you?" Bastian's form tensed.

"Yeah. I mean, he didn't introduce himself as the century-old benefactor of a curse, but he did tell me his name."

"It's not a coincidence. He knows who you are. He's dangerous, Odette."

"What could he do to me?" They were still part of a civilized society, were they not?

If it was possible, Bastian's face paled.

"You think he would kill me?" Odette's stomach churned. She felt like she might throw up.

"He wouldn't think twice," Bastian replied.

The dim room tilted and started to spin. Odette closed her eyes and counted her breaths.

"I can't have you risking your life for me," Bastian said as he closed the space between them.

Odette blinked the world back into focus. She shook her head, shaking off the last bits of dizziness and Bastian's statement. "You don't get to make that decision for me."

"Then I'll make it for myself. I don't want your help anymore." Bastian turned and walked toward his piano.

"So you're just giving up?" Odette followed.

"It's not giving up." Bastian ran his fingers over the ivory keys. "It's accepting my fate."

Odette resisted the urge to shut the lid on his hands to get him to look at her. "If you were supposed to accept it, I wouldn't be able to see you. That isn't how this works."

He sat down on the dusty bench. Quiet. Calm. "How can you be so sure?"

"How can you be so *unsure*?" She sat beside him and, while her voice lowered, the pace of her heart did not. It took everything in her not to rant at his cowardice…even if it was born out of concern for her. "I'm not sure if you're aware, but I'm not the type of person to just let things go."

"I don't deserve the type of person you are." Bastian played two soft notes.

Odette reached for his hand. The keys tinkled. She squeezed his cool fingers in her right hand while her left lifted to his face, grazing his cheek.

Bastian leaned into her touch.

"There is good in you, Bastian. I've seen it even if you want to forget it. I can't and I won't." She tilted his chin up.

For the first time since stepping onto his stage, Bastian looked into Odette's face. His eyes glistened as tears escaped his grasp and dripped down his see-through cheeks. "I can't let anyone else get hurt because of me."

"You deserve a chance to breathe in this world." Her voice quivered as her tears wet her face. "I want to help give you that chance—to give you a life that's beautiful to witness—and I am well aware of the risk."

Bastian sighed. "Is there anything I can say that will change your mind?"

"Nope."

Hesitantly, he reached for her, wiping her tears with his thumb. "Please be careful."

A charge prickled under his touch. Treacherous indeed. This was the real danger. This—sitting centimeters away from him, feeling his skin and breath while he was not yet real—this is what would break her if she failed. She almost leaned into it, gave in to it.

"Anything for you, ghost-boy," she said. Willpower pulled her back from him at an excruciatingly slow pace.

"Not a ghost." His whisper was so low and his eyes so longing, she almost didn't hear his standard reply.

She let go of his hand with one last squeeze. "Not for long."

# CHAPTER 32
## OCTAVIAN

Octavian flipped up the collar of his jacket as a chilly rain began to fall over the city. Mingled with the nightlife, he had followed Odette from the cafe to the theater to her apartment, amused when she would look back only to see nothing and no one behind her.

One learns things over a century. Remaining hidden when you don't wish to be seen had been one of Octavian's greatest lessons taught to him by pickpockets in the nineteen-thirties of London. Bastian had wanted the spotlight, but Octavian didn't procure the curse out of some desire for celebrity. Of all the things he loved about life, a world of selfies and viral videos wasn't one of them. Fame was a poor man's fulfillment. He had desired the richness and freedom of time and wealth and knowledge and power. Real power didn't need the flash of photographers. No, Octavian revealed himself when and how he wanted. No more. No less.

Token moments spent with Odette were calculated. A look, a laugh, a question was all he needed to measure this woman who was putting a wrench in his immortality. She was unassuming, intelligent, and seemed to be developing feelings for Bastian.

Octavian's stomach lurched at the thought. He tossed his

half-drunk Earl Grey into the nearest garbage bin and took a left at the corner. With Odette tucked securely into her apartment, he had other business to attend to. Two more left turns and a right took him to the door of *Barbot's Tinctures and Tonics*.

The hinges squeaked.

"Sorry, we are closing up. You'll have to come back tomorrow!" Meg called from the back room.

Octavian closed the door and turned the OPEN sign along with the lock. "Oh, I think you'll make an exception."

Octavian never tired of the flinch of fear which crossed Meg's face every time she saw him. He drank in the intoxication of the hold he had over her. It was the same hold he'd had over Juleanne. Generations twitching and anxious over what he might do.

"I hope you have something of worth to share with me." Octavian ran a hand through the growing gray streak in his hair. He showed Meg his wrinkled hands. "I am running out of time and patience."

"I don't have anything to tell you." She touched a hand to the pocket of her denim pants.

"I don't think that's true."

Octavian stepped toward Meg, and she stepped backward. He reached for her arm, and she leaned away. It was an uncomfortable and tense dance between them, but he was leading and closing the space.

He gripped her shoulder, digging fingers in just enough for her to squirm. "Show me," he nodded toward her pocket.

Meg jerked away. "It's nothing."

"Show. Me." Octavian growled.

Meg pulled a folded page and held it out to him with trembling hands.

Octavian seized it. Unfolding the paper revealed a now wrinkled photo of Juleanne. He studied it, searching for what made it special enough to hide. In the top corner, scribbled in blue ink, were the words, *Is this Bastian's ring?*

It was Bastian's ring, which meant Juleanne had kept it, which meant it could be retrieved. But the ring was less important at the moment than the handwriting. It wasn't Meg's—he had seen her penmanship, with its elegant, flowery loops. This was a messy mix of graceful lines and squished scribbles.

"She was here." The realization snuck out under his breath.

"I don't know what you're talking about," Meg said. She retreated behind the counter; closing up jars, tucking receipts into folders, and refusing to make eye contact.

"Oh, you know exactly what and who I am talking about." Octavian placed the printed image in front of her. "Odette Durand brought you this. Why?"

Meg reached to pick up the photo but stopped herself, choosing instead to place her hands in her back pockets. "She is looking for the ring, same as you. And I told her what I told you; I don't know where it is."

"But *you* are also looking for it. Did you tell her that?"

"I didn't tell her anything else. I swear."

"Good girl. See that it stays that way." Octavian tapped a finger on the picture. "And do find this ring for me. I'm giving you forty-eight hours."

"Then what?" Meg's question bore no defiance in its tone, just a quiver of apprehension.

"I'll tell you just like I told Juleanne," he drawled with a smirk, "let's not find out what exactly I am capable of…for your child's sake."

# CHAPTER 33
# ODETTE

Odette found it nearly impossible to focus on anything work-related after yesterday; the visit to *Barbot's* the previous night, Meg's genuine fear, seeing Octavian, discovering who he really was from Bastian. She was failing in her attempts to input new inventory into Isabelle's outdated computer system. And her mocha was cold. Again.

She left her post at the front counter to reheat the latte. She watched it spin behind the glass of the microwave door while the little clock counted down the seconds.

Just as her mocha was freshly heated, the front door chimed.

"Odette!" Isabelle called from the entry. "I have the mail and exciting events abound!"

Odette sipped her now warmed up drink as she returned to the counter where Isabelle had plopped down a pile of mail, abandoning it all for a black envelope decorated in a silver filagree and closed with crimson wax.

"It has finally arrived," Isabelle said. She took her gold letter opener and carefully peeled back the wax to maintain the integrity of the beautiful seal. She lifted the flap and then slid out the contents. The stationary matched its enclosure. Isabelle put on her reading glasses and perused the shimmering lettering, a whimsical smile lighting her face.

"What is it?" Odette wondered with her own amount of awe drawn just from the older woman's delight.

"My darling, this is an invitation to the biggest event in the Quarter; the annual Masquerade Ball." Isabelle handed Odette the invite.

"The one from the photo?" Odette peered at the memory board on the wall behind her.

"Yes!" Isabelle said. "It's held in the grandest mansion in the whole French Quarter. I have gone nearly every year, and this year you are going to be my plus one!"

Odette read over the details. "It's in just two days?"

"Waiting until the last minute to send the invitations is part of the charm," Isabelle said. "Dates back to the first ball, which was given by some famous architect to celebrate the birth of his son before heading off to fight in the Civil War or some such thing. The point is, it's a wonderful time and you are going with me."

"Do I even get a say in this?"

"No," Isabelle laughed and headed toward the kitchenette in the back. "I'm going to make a cup of tea and we will sit and talk about what to wear."

Half of Odette thought now was not the time for balls and dancing, but the other half argued she could use the distraction. Given that Isabelle would be on the side of the latter, Odette knew there was no point in continuing her internal debate and chose instead to surrender. She grabbed the rest of the mail as she headed toward the velvet chairs.

"Now, I don't want you to worry about buying anything," Isabelle said as she sat down. "I have plenty of ballgowns you could choose from…in every color."

"I don't want to impose…"

"Nonsense! Consider my wardrobe as your wardrobe." Isabelle sipped her tea. "I have a red number I think would be perfect for you. Oh, and a blue one. And black!"

Odette giggled. "I am sure any one of them will be beautiful."

"You should come over to my apartment after work and try them on. I have plenty of masks too, from previous years. We'll play dress-up like proper society women."

"You do love this ball."

"Oh yes." Isabelle relaxed into her chair, closing her eyes and sighing. "It's always a magical and mystical kind of night, full of dancing and dreaming and falling in love."

Odette didn't miss the insinuation dripping from the word love. She was about to protest the idea, but the image of Bastian in a tuxedo flashed through her mind. So she opted for a long sip of her mocha instead. Thankfully Isabelle didn't continue down that meddling path, though the gleam in her eye proved she was indeed restraining herself.

"Here's the rest of the mail." Odette handed it over to be sure the subject changed.

Isabelle flipped through the stack. "Bill. Bill. Junk. Scam. Bill. There's nothing else fun in here. Ah, but here's a note for you."

Isabelle handed her a small white envelope. It had no postage or address. Just a gold *fleur de lis* layered over a capital B on one side and Odette's name scribbled in black ink on the other.

"Thank you," Odette said. She pulled a folded piece of paper from the envelope.


*Odette,*

*I think I can help you after all. I'll be at the annual masquerade ball and, if you can manage to meet me in the courtyard, I think we can avoid suspicion. Find me there after nine, wearing a red dress and matching mask with black jewels and feathers on both sides. But approach carefully. Eyes are watching, remember?*

*Meg*


• • •

It was serendipity or sovereignty. Even if Odette would decline Isabelle's invitation, she couldn't say no to this one. Her mind buzzed about what this could mean for Bastian and breaking his curse. It could all be for nothing, or it could be the key to everything.

# CHAPTER 34
## BASTIAN

Bastian had spent the past twenty-four tortuous hours dissuading himself from dreaming of what could be with Odette. With every touch of her skin on his, hope had grown in his heart, but then his mind would dash it away. He could bear an eternity of oblivion easier than he could bear the disappointment and heartbreak that would come if all the dreaming and hoping failed…or harmed her.

"Your problem is you still worry that you deserve all this." Sister Mary Cecilia changed out the vase of wilted roses like she did every three days.

"Don't I?"

The nun sighed. "Does it matter?" She paused in her floral arranging, thoughtfulness crinkling her already wrinkled face. "Love isn't based on merit. Neither love for others nor our love for ourselves, and certainly not the Maker's love for us." She studied the red rose in her hand, sniffed its fragrant velvet petals, and then placed it in the glass jar. "I don't know who you were one hundred years ago, but I see who you are now. How I wish you could see you as I do."

Bastian had argued the same case with the sister a thousand times. Her faith and devotion had given her a sense of the world he hadn't felt. His vision had been clouded with self-pity and fear for so long. Trying to have faith now took an energy he didn't know how long he could sustain.

"Bastian?" His name floated from backstage as Odette slipped through the ragged curtains. "Oh, hello Sister."

"Hello, dearie," Mary Cecelia said.

Odette held up a small white envelope and folded paper. "I told you we have an ally, and she has news that will help us."

Bastian replied with a trickle of piano notes.

"What's wrong with him?" Odette whispered to the nun.

"He's in a mood…again," Sister Mary Cecilia replied.

"Well, snap out of it, ghost-boy." Odette sat next to him on the piano bench, showing him the correspondence from Meg.

"I'm not a ghost," Bastian reminded her. He perused the page Odette held out for him to read. "Who is Meg?"

"She's the owner of *Barbot's Tonics and Tinctures…*"

"Barbot?" There was something familiar in the name. "Odette, you need to be careful with—"

"Yeah, we've had that talk already," Odette said. "I'm certain Octavian has Meg scared too, but she's willing to help and I'm going to let her, and you're going to let me, because…well, it's not like you can stop us."

"I like her more and more," Sister Mary Cecilia giggled.

"I wish she would listen to me," Bastian grumbled.

"I listen," Odette said. "I just do what I want anyway. I'm a strong, independent woman, Bas. I can handle a hundred-year-old southern charmer."

Bastian's brain bounced between the endearment of his shortened name and frustration at her stubbornness. "Is there any voice of reason you will listen to?"

"No." Odette stuffed the note into her bag.

"I give up," Bastian said.

"Don't give up, just give in," Sister Mary Cecilia said.

"I like her more and more." Odette laughed. She tucked a strand of hair behind her ears and pushed her glasses up on her nose. "And...I'd like it if you came to the masquerade ball tomorrow night."

Odette's cheeks flushed a dusty pink and she didn't meet his gaze. When she did finally glance at him, he looked away quickly, feeling like an awkward teenager.

"Odette, I..." Bastian struggled to pull one of the ten thoughts swirling in his head and turn it into a response.

"I just think you should be close by when Meg shares her information, you know, in case it's time-sensitive or something..."

Bastian touched her hand to halt her explanations. "I don't think it's a good idea, Odette. I can't..." He couldn't be seen. He couldn't dance with her. He couldn't stand to be surrounded by reminders of what he couldn't have and would never be. "I think it's best to just meet me back here after if there is anything worth sharing." He pulled his hand away.

"I think you should get over yourself and crash this big fancy ball while you're invisible and have the luxury." Odette stood up and started to leave. She stopped next to the nun. "Maybe you can convince him."

"Bastian isn't easily convinced of anything, dearie." Sister Mary Cecilia smiled at the girl and patted her arm.

Odette exited stage left the same way she had entered.

Bastian stood up and sulked in the same direction, then paced back toward the piano, stopping next to the nun.

"You should go to the ball," she said.

"Are you my fairy godmother now? Will there be a pumpkin?"

"You will be the pumpkin if you don't go to that ball and see her all dressed up and lovely."

"What good will it do?" Bastian scoffed. "Will she dance with a phantom until the stroke of midnight and then remember I'm mostly dead and this is all useless?"

"Nothing done to help another soul is useless, Bastian." Sister

Mary Cecilia gathered her basket of dry, faded flowers. "Go to the ball. She is here for you. Be there for her."

Bastian was silent as the nun left. He was usually comfortable in his loneliness, but just now it was suffocating. His lungs burned for something more than oxygen and his heart once again wanted to reach for the hope of a dream that might leave him broken. Perhaps broken was better than invisible. Better than forgotten.

He pulled at his haphazard hair, then spun on his heel and pounded a fist against the top of the dusty grand piano.

The roses rattled. A crimson petal floated down and settled on the ebony surface. Words the nun had spoken to him not that long ago drifted to the front of his dreary thoughts; *You are not cut off from the vine.*

# CHAPTER 35
# ODETTE

Odette spent an hour trying on every dress Isabelle had. Not because she needed to or even wanted to, but because the older woman had insisted. She said the only way Odette could be sure to find the perfect dress was to see all the imperfect ones. She also said that the same advice was not applicable when it came to dating. "Imperfect dresses won't break your heart but imperfect men...ha!" She had laughed while zipping up the back of a blue frock with feathers hanging off the fringe.

When all was said and done, Isabelle's room was a mess of fabric strewn about the large four-post bed and chenille chaise lounge, but Odette had her gown for the ball—complete with matching shoes and a mask—wrapped up in a gray garment bag. She offered her gratitude and a promise to Isabelle to take good care of the items before she left and started toward home.

It was a no-brainer to pop into Madame Clary's to grab a bite to eat. Her stomach growled at the smell of dinnertime wafting through the busy streets.

"And what do we have here?" Lizzie cooed from behind the counter, pointing to the garment bag folded over Odette's arm.

"Isabelle is letting me borrow a gown for the ball," Odette said.

"I bet you are going to look beautiful...be the belle of the ball..."

"I'm not sure about that, but it is a gorgeous dress." Odette thought for a moment of her reflection in Isabelle's full-length mirror. The frock had made her feel quite grand. She wondered if Bastian would agree.

*Stop it, Odette. You can't keep dreaming about ghost-boy.*

"Everything okay?" Lizzie asked.

"Yes." Odette quickly shifted her thoughts away from Bastian and onto food. "What's good today?"

"Our special is pretty good, if I do say so myself; a smoked turkey panini with swiss."

"I'll take one to go."

"Joe! Get our girl a special!"

"On it!" Joe shouted from the kitchen.

"It'll be just a minute," Lizzie said.

Before Odette could even nod, a chill tickled the back of her neck. She turned toward the open door, thinking a breeze had been let in, but found none other than Octavian Zane standing just four feet behind her. She jerked back around, blinking rapidly and inhaling a deep breath to settle the anxiety rising in her chest.

Lizzie's brow furrowed, and she pursed her lips. "You sure you're okay?"

Odette swallowed. "Yeah, I'm fine. Promise." She did her best to offer a smile that would convince the owner, but the suspicion on Lizzie's face didn't lift.

"Order up!" Joe shouted, passing a brown bag through the pass-through window.

Lizzie grabbed it and handed it to Odette with a deep sigh. "You know if you need anything..."

"I know," Odette replied, taking the bag. "I know." She repeated the response as much for herself as Lizzie.

When she turned to leave, Zane was staring right at her. Whatever charm he'd exuded before had dissolved. Odette couldn't be sure if it was just her imagination, but he seemed to have aged at least ten years. There were dark circles under his eyes. The gray streak in his hair had widened. And the smirk on his face only made him appear villainous.

"Good day, Miss Odette," he drawled and tipped his head. "Aren't you looking lovely this evening?"

Odette wanted to gag. Had she really swooned before? Would she swoon now if she didn't know the truth? Zane was well-dressed and polished in every way. He had the etiquette of a fine Southern gentleman. But under the surface, he was selfish and terrible. It was a lesson that fairytales often tried to teach— fairytales and her old Sunday School teacher, Mrs. Lynn—looks could be deceiving. It was so easy to judge by outward appearances and first impressions. But if beauty was found within, Octavian Zane wasn't the handsome hero, but the hideous beast.

"Good day," Odette muttered before sweeping past Zane and out of the cafe.

Once on the street, she shuddered. Anxiety mingled with anger in a hot tingle under her skin. Suddenly, her brain buzzed with all the things she wanted to say to that man. She had half a mind to march right back into that cafe and tell him she knew exactly who he was and what he had done. To let him know all the ways he was deficient and fragile and weak. But she wouldn't. Partly because it would not be smart to antagonize her enemy. Second, because fairytales and Mrs. Lynn had also taught her that the difference between heroes and villains was a small sliver of brokenness where the evil was allowed to seep in. She didn't need to fight Octavian Zane. He was probably already warring with himself.

# CHAPTER 36

# ODETTE

Odette stared at the ball gown hanging from her bedroom door. She was warm and comfortable on her couch and under her soft blanket. Hepburn was cozy against her legs. Clouds were blocking the morning sun and keeping the room wonderfully dim as a light rain pattered against the metal balcony. It was the perfect day to stay in sweatpants and watch episodes of her favorite shows. She could order takeout and not even leave her apartment.

Except she couldn't.

Tonight, she had a ball to attend, a mostly dead jazz musician to save, and a curse to break. It was quite the eclectic to-do list. She was losing her nerve to complete it...if she even could.

Two days ago, she was nothing but excited and impassioned by the prospect of Meg's news and helping Bastian. But today was the day and excitement had been replaced with a low hum of apprehension.

"Can I really do this?" Odette asked her cat as much as herself. Part of her hoped the cat would suddenly have some miraculous counsel, but Hepburn only grumbled under her breath in response.

"I guess if I want advice, I'm going to have to go to someone who can talk."

A short walk later, Odette shook the drizzle from her green umbrella before stepping inside the cafe. She had hoped the place would be less busy, but perhaps tables full of chatting patrons were a sign that she should just buy a latte and go back home. Maybe she should hibernate in her apartment until ghosts no longer existed again and villains were only in storybooks.

"Good mor—What's wrong?" Lizzie began.

If Odette had ever held the power to hide her emotions and look like everything was fine when her insides felt otherwise, Lizzie was her kryptonite. "I'm fine…" She began, but her chest trembled and wet eyes betrayed her attempt at assurance.

"Oh, darlin', go have a seat." Lizzie pointed to an empty table in the back corner. "I'll grab us some coffee and be right there."

Odette nodded and obeyed.

She hung her purse on the back of the chair and leaned her damp umbrella against the table legs before having a seat. A chill of anxiety made her shudder.

"There you go." Lizzie set down two large mugs topped with steamed milk and then sat across from Odette. "Tell me what's the matter." She offered comfort with a warm smile and a pat on Odette's hand.

"Honestly, I'm just scared," Odette blurted. She didn't have the time or energy to beat around the bush, especially with Lizzie.

"There are different kinds of scared. Can you be a little more specific?"

Odette sipped the warm latte, gathering her thoughts on how best she should explain this. "I need to do a hard thing to help someone…"

"Is this the someone we talked about before?"

Odette nodded. "I want to help him. I think I can help him.

But it involves at least a little risk." It could be outright danger-ous, but she held back so as not to have to explain all the super-natural elements of this endeavor.

"Well…" Lizzie laced her fingers together and took a deep breath. "Lots of worthwhile things in life involve risk. The key is using wisdom to determine if it's a worthwhile risk. Does the good that you could do outweigh the possible bad? Is it moti-vated by love?"

"I think it does." Odette paused for a moment to still the butterflies swarming in her stomach. "And I think it is."

"Then you pray on it to be sure. Because I can't tell you what to do, but the Source of all wisdom can." Lizzie leaned back and smiled again, her face lighting up in a way that exuded a joy and peace that didn't quite make sense to Odette. Lizzie sighed and continued, "What I can tell you is that hard things are often scary but also good. We can't let fear control us and steal away the good that can be done."

Odette took another long sip of her latte. Her mother had always told her to be safe, not scared. *We have to be aware of the danger without being stifled by our fear of it.* But Odette wasn't just afraid of Octavian or of being hurt by him, she was also afraid of failing Bastian. She was afraid of succeeding and finding out what that would mean. Would it mean losing him forever? Would it mean getting to keep him? Wasn't it another ghost-boy who asked a similar question in a movie she loved when she was a kid?

Now wasn't the time to get nostalgic for *Casper*, not when real ghosts were counting on her.

"Besides, fear is a liar," Lizzie continued, pulling Odette back to the conversation. "It can tell us we are more important than we actually are or that we aren't important at all. Either way, it usually steers us wrong. Except in the case of snakes, spiders, and haunted houses." Lizzie chuckled at herself, then leaned in again. "You can't stop being afraid, but don't let fear be the moti-vator. Let love do that, and I think you'll be all right."

*Love*. It seemed a bit of a farce in this situation. The whole thing held an absurdity others would find unbelievable. Yet here she was, hearing the music, seeing Bastian, and attempting to break curses like a regular fairytale heroine. Why not just admit her heart was in play and not just her head?

"Thank you," Odette said. "I'm glad I came here and I'm glad we talked."

"Me too," Lizzie replied. "I told you I'm here to talk anytime you need it. That's what family does."

"Thank you for that, too." For the first time in a few days, Odette felt light enough to let herself smile a real smile. "For being family."

Lizzie stood up and came behind Odette, wrapping her in a hug. "And in the spirit of family, let me make you a sandwich."

Odette relished the embrace and laughed. "I will never turn down your food."

# CHAPTER 37
# ODETTE

Floating lights sparkled like stars over moonlit walkways as Odette stood outside the grand house. Music wafted through the tall glass windows and the large door that lay open, revealing the warm glow inside. She slipped her shimmery, black lace mask over her face and stepped over the threshold. The room smelled of sweet gardenias and roasted hors d'oeuvres. The aromas floated through a neighboring doorway and mingled with the melody of the jazz band to circle Odette. She let her senses carry her forward from the foyer into the bustling ballroom.

It was already filled with people in tuxedos and flowing dresses, all wearing masks adorned with feathers, ribbons, and jewels whose shimmer was lost to the glimmer of the grand chandelier which hung from the center of the ceiling, dangling with hundreds of crystals. It seemed to dance and sway just like the patrons beneath it who twirled around on the dance floor.

Tall, tapered candles sat in silver candelabras, their flames flickering on every table bordering the large hall. Odette spotted Isabelle near the far corner and made her way through the crowd, being careful not to catch any of the beads on her black dress.

"You look stunning!" Isabelle stood and held out her hands as Odette approached. "I knew that art deco number was the perfect choice."

"You were right," Odette replied. She had felt like a star straight out of the golden age of movies as she had twirled in front of her mirror earlier that evening. The luxurious fabric hugged her figure before flaring around her feet. A pattern of onyx beads crisscrossed over the bodice while matching strands dangled from shear-capped sleeves. Gold T-strap heels peeked from under the hem matching the beaded choker around her delicate neck. Odette wasn't much for fancy clothes, but she couldn't deny how glamorous she felt. "Thank you again for letting me borrow it…and for letting me be your plus one."

"You are most welcome, but don't you dare spend the whole evening over here next to me. Mingle. Flirt. Dance. Fall in love!"

"How about I start with something to drink and see where the night takes me from there?" Odette said with a laugh.

"As long as you enjoy yourself." Isabelle squeezed her fingers and then caught sight of someone she knew and, with a smile and a wave, flitted away.

Odette turned her attention toward the waiters lapping the room while she waited for Meg. The thought of their meeting and what news Meg would bring brought goosebumps down Odette's bare arms. She snagged a sparkling drink from a silver tray and took a sip, the bubbly liquid cooling her dry throat. Her head and heart buzzed as she whispered a prayer. Isabelle said the night of the ball was always magical, but she didn't need magic so much as a miracle. Perhaps Meg would come bearing miracles.

"You look enchanting," someone drawled behind Odette.

She felt a hand on her bare shoulder and turned to look directly at Octavian Zane. "Thank you." She dipped ever so slightly away from his touch.

"It seems a travesty that someone as beautiful as you would be standing here alone." His devilish grin darkened his features.

Odette noticed that even more gray had appeared since the last time they'd met.

"I'm perfectly fine here," Odette said. She took another sip from her glass.

"Well, then perhaps you would accompany me to the dance floor as a kindness?"

"I'm not sure…".

Octavian took the glass from her hand and set it on the nearby cocktail table. "I must insist."

Odette swallowed a bitter taste and nodded. She accepted Octavian's hand and he led her out amid waltzing couples. She touched his shoulder and shuddered when his hand lay against her back.

"I know you see him," Zane whispered.

His warm breath made her skin crawl and her stomach lurch. He must know her involvement. Had Meg betrayed her? She could deny everything, act oblivious to the story she had found herself in. But lying didn't suit her, and neither did cowardice.

"Yes, I can see Bastian."

"The next logical question would be why, but I really don't care. See him all you want. Talk to him. Take walks to the bridge…" he leaned in closer, squeezing her hand just beyond what was comfortable. "But forget any foolhardy notion you have of saving him."

"That sounds like a threat," Odette replied. Her mind was whirling over exactly how much Octavian might have seen. She knew he'd been watching, but she hadn't realized his observation of her had been that close.

"It's more than that. It is a promise, my dear." Octavian twirled her away, then roughly back into his arms. "One I would rather not keep, but I can't let even you…" he caressed her cheek with the back of his hand. "And your sweet face, get in the way of my immortality."

Odette turned away from his touch and his gaze. She wriggled, trying to create some distance between them.

"Is everything okay here?" Isabelle interrupted the tension.

"Completely," Zane replied. He released Odette and stepped backward, bowing slightly. "Thank you for the dance, Odette. I do hope it's the last one we share." He sauntered away, disappearing into the crowd.

"What was that about?" Isabelle asked.

"I guess not all southern gentlemen are gentlemen," Odette replied with a tremor in her chest.

"I truly do not like that man," Isabelle said.

"Neither do I," Odette said. "I think I need a moment to freshen up."

"Of course." Isabelle patted her hand and smiled softly. "Of course."

Odette skittered across the room and through the gauzy white curtains and French doors onto the veranda. She inhaled chilly air and breathed it out in a translucent puff. She squeezed her fingers into fists and then released them as she leaned her head back to stare into the navy sky. Stars flickered. The moon stared down, full and bright. Standing in the stream of its light, she whispered a prayer asking for peace to wash away her anxiety.

"Are you all right?"

Odette spun at the sound of Bastian's soft voice. "I am now." The sentiment escaped her before she'd had a chance to disguise the honesty with wit.

Bastian rarely really smiled. She'd discovered that pretty quickly. It was like smiles were signs of hope that he was careful not to latch onto. His smiles were secrets that started in his eyes —a light that brightened his demeanor before his lips ever curved—but when they did, it was a slow curl, ever so slight at first, then breaking free and pushing his cheeks upward. She adored his smile. Especially when it was pointed at her.

"You look…" Bastian licked his bottom lip. "Beautiful.

Odette's cheeks warmed as she ran her hand over the soft waves of her hair that draped over her left shoulder.

Bastian stepped closer, his ear inclined toward the notes of soft music reaching the vacant courtyard. He held out his hand. "Care to dance?"

Odette reached for him, their fingers meeting with a spark. "I'd love to."

Bastian pulled her against him. The feel of him, his nearness, was this odd static mix of warm and cold. It tingled all over, like the meeting of flesh and bone with something utterly supernatural. When his hand rested against the small of her back, it sent shivers up her spine. Not like Octavian. Her senses weren't filling with apprehension, but serenity.

Odette leaned her cheek against Bastian's as they silently waltzed about the patio garden. She knew if anyone walked outside, it would appear as though she was dancing with herself and would look at least mildly insane. But Odette didn't care. She was tired of trying to appear sane. Let the whole world think she was crazy. If just for this moment, let them see and let them judge. For one moment, one dance under the watching moon, Odette would let herself be honest with her own heart. She loved Bastian Roux. And his presence, along with the thump of his heart against hers, told her that he loved her too.

# CHAPTER 38

# BASTIAN

Bastian could spend another hundred years locked in this moment with Odette. Clinging to her warmth. Inhaling the sweet lilac scent of her perfume. With her in his arms, he felt like he could survive anything, do anything, be anything. Holding her, touching her, it watered the dry desert of hope that lay in the depths of his heart. It was taking root. It was sprouting, breaking through the surface of his ever-present fear.

The taste of it—of love—both satiated his worry and stirred it, like waves lapping the shore, ferocious and calming at the same time. Dancing with her made him want to dive all the way in.

"I thought you weren't going to come." Odette's breath warmed Bastian's cheek.

"I wasn't," he replied. "But I realized I—"

"You're here," a voice interrupted Bastian's confession.

Odette pulled away. The air around him cooled except for his hand, which was still tangled with hers.

"Meg," Odette said.

"Not here," the woman in a red velvet dress replied. She pulled the feathered mask from her face and there was a familiarity to her features. It was just barely a notion to Bastian. She ushered them into a dark corner of the courtyard where the light and watching eyes from the windows didn't reach.

"Bastian, this is Juleanne's great-granddaughter, Meg. She's been helping me try to figure out how to break the curse her grandmother enacted…Octavian's curse." Odette added the last line with some sort of purpose in her voice. Perhaps to keep him from turning any anger on the young woman before him.

"He's here?" Meg's eyes widened, then she squinted like she was trying to find some evidence of his presence.

"I'd say hello, but…"

Meg gasped.

"You heard that?" Odette asked.

"That's impossible," Bastian said.

"Things are changing. She believes, so…" Odette shrugged and squeezed his hand.

"Whatever I heard, we don't have time to discuss it. Octavian is still inside. He's currently caught in a dance with some rich socialite. But…"

"What have you found?" Bastian asked, cutting off Meg's worries, which would only add further flame to the anxiety blooming in his chest.

"I found a great auntie who remembered the ring," Meg began.

"And?" Bastian could barely contain his nerves.

"And they buried her with it," Meg replied. "Here are the details for her crypt. Go there. Open it. Retrieve your ring."

"Then what?" Odette asked as she took the folded paper from Meg. "Throw it into the fires of Mount Doom?"

Meg stifled a soft laugh. "I don't think it will take a quest through Middle Earth, but fire might not be a bad idea."

"I don't understand," Bastian whispered, trying to make sense of all the unfamiliar words and references he'd just heard.

"I made a witty movie reference that I can explain later. For now, we go melt that ring," Odette said then turned her focus back to Meg. "And destroying the ring will break Bastian's curse?"

Meg inhaled deeply and bit her bottom lip. She seemed hesitant to look Odette in the eye. "I don't do voodoo. No one in my family has since Juleanne. I just sell herbal remedies. Destroying the ring is the best solution I could find, for whatever that's worth. I can't say it will work, and I can't tell you what way it will go for your Bastian if it does—renewed life or just final death."

Odette squeezed Bastian's trembling hand.

It wasn't new information. They had always known breaking the curse had multiple potential outcomes. Either one meant Bastian's freedom. But only one meant Odette. When had that come to matter more to him?

Applause erupted from inside the ballroom as the dance ended.

"You need to go now." Meg glanced toward the doorway.

"Come with us," Odette said.

"I can't. He can't know I helped you." Meg's jaw quivered. She looked over her shoulder again. "I'm going to sneak away. I'll give you the night, but I'll have to tell him in the morning, or…or he'll…"

"I understand." Odette shared a knowing look with Meg then hugged her quickly. "Go."

Meg nodded, lifting her mask back over her face before stepping back inside the ballroom.

"This is it." Odette turned to him and touched a hand to Bastian's cheek. An unsure smile curved her pink lips.

"Are you sure you still want to do this?" He couldn't hide his apprehension. "There will be no going back."

"You deserve to be free of this, no matter what," Odette said.

Bastian turned away from her and gazed upward into the heavens. "What if I'm not worthy of it?"

Odette grabbed his chin and pulled his gaze back to her masked eyes. "Everyone is worthy of a redemption arc. Even melancholy ghost-boys." She leaned closer on tiptoes, eyes fluttering closed, and her lips grazed his in a soft, sweet kiss. She lingered close for the length of a warm breath, then tugged him toward the garden gate.

"I'm not a ghost, you know."

She looked back over her shoulder. Her face was glowing with a light he was sure couldn't be coming from outside. "I know," she said and pulled him forward faster.

# CHAPTER 39

# ODETTE

O dette knocked on the abbey door. A light flipped on inside. She could hear shuffling steps just before the knob turned, and the door opened.

"What are you doing here all dressed up? Shouldn't you be dancing the night away?" Sister Mary Cecelia said, wiping her hand on a kitchen towel. "I just baked some cookies to bring to the children's home and I'm sure I can spare one or two if you'd like to come in." She opened the door wider.

"While I am tempted by fresh-baked cookies, they will have to wait. We found out where the ring is," Odette gushed. "We can break Bastian's curse." She tried to control her tapping feet.

"Oh my, what wonderful news! How?" The sister said.

"It involves a trip to the cemetery and destroying a ring. Wanna come?" Odette wasn't quite sure why everything was coming out of her mouth with such excitement when her insides were screaming every worst-case scenario one could think of. "But, it could be dangerous so..."

"I certainly wouldn't miss being there when Bastian's curse is broken." She tossed the towel on the nearby table and stepped outside. "Are we taking the trolley? Because my old-lady legs aren't made for that kind of walking."

"The trolley it is," Odette said, then turned to Bastian, who had been standing silently behind her. She couldn't read his face. It held the same muddle of emotions she was feeling. Flashes of joy and terror all mingled together in his misty eyes and wavering smiles.

Neither Odette, the nun, nor Bastian uttered a word in the relatively empty streetcar. There was everything and nothing to say and each stop seemed to take an eternity making the thirty-minute ride feel like it held lifetimes worth of anticipation and apprehension. Odette imagined the route like a quest montage from a movie where the adventurers sat horseback along moun-tain ridges or trudged through snow and mud on their way to slay dragons. Epic music would have played in the background. Instead, there was the quiet hum of some pop radio station and the chatter of passengers getting on and off.

Finally, they disembarked at their solemn destination. The cemetery was a grid of walkways between mausoleums and crypts. Odette understood now why locals referred to them as cities of the dead. They were entire consecrated neighborhoods filled with final resting places, all of them adorned with crosses, angelic statues, and wilted flowers. Each little home was built of granite, marble, or brick. Most had become weathered over the years and were covered in a layer of grime. Names of their resi-dents were fading, and weeds poked through cracks in the sidewalk.

Odette's dress swished with each step she took under the dim light of lamps that lined the path. Some candles glinted near a few graves, creating creeping, dancing shadows keeping vigil. Odette shivered.

She looked at the note Meg had given her. "It's this way...I think."

Sister Mary Cecilia touched her arm. "There is no need to fear the dead." The nun smiled and marched forward without a flinch at the misty fog crawling over the ground.

"She's right," Bastian said, taking Odette's hand.

They weaved their way right and then left, until they came to a rectangular mausoleum with an arched roof. Moss and vines grew along the dilapidated granite columns that stood sentinel in front of a rusted iron door marked with a fleur de lis. Above it read the name *BARBOT*.

"This is it," Odette said, noticing dying roses and corroded coins strewn in front of the entry like it was a shrine.

With more than a little trepidation, Odette opened the door. Every horror movie scenario she had ever seen flashed through her mind. "If Lara Croft can do this, so can I."

"Who is Lara Croft?" Bastian whispered close behind her.

"When this is over, I am making a must-see list, and we are having a movie marathon posthaste. Film and TV references are vital parts of healthy communication in my book," Odette said.

She ducked inside the small tomb. What little light was offered by streetlamps didn't reach inside the windowless room. She pulled her cell phone out of her small, beaded purse and turned on the flashlight. Dust particles floated like forest wisps in the stream of bright, white light. Cobwebs hung from the ceiling like little veils, covering niches of urns in all shapes and sizes. In the center of the room was a coffin-shaped crypt. It was so large compared to the size of the tomb that it almost made it impossible to walk around. On the top, Odette saw that it was inscribed; *Juleanne Barbot, 1846-1938.*

"I take it from your staring that the ring is in there." Sister Mary Cecilia pointed to the large stone box.

"Yep," Odette said.

"Or so we were told," Bastian added.

"This city is too superstitious to set traps using a voodoo queen's grave," Sister Mary Cecilia said. "So I say let's get it opened." She picked up a discarded lighter sitting on a corner table. It clicked and sputtered as she began to light the melted pillar candles set about the shelves and floor.

Odette turned off her phone in exchange for the warmer glow of flickering flames. She gripped the granite lid and made an effort to lift it with little success. "Did anyone think to pack a crowbar?"

"Let's try less lifting and more pushing." The sister stood beside Odette and together they pushed.

"If you can touch piano keys and break vases, you can at least *attempt* to help us," Odette said with a pointed stare in Bastian's direction.

"So I'm *not* a ghost when it benefits you?" He asked and then smirked and stepped up to join the two women.

"Just try," Odette retorted.

With huffs and grunts, the three shoved against the heavy cover until it finally began to inch forward, little by little, revealing desiccated remains that were little more than a pile of ash.

"We need more light." Sister Mary Cecilia retrieved a dripping candle and held it over the six-inch opening they had managed to secure.

Odette and Bastian leaned to peer inside. Something glinted gold in the candlelight.

Odette inhaled a deep, dusty breath. She had resolved herself to the fact she might have to touch a corpse to retrieve the ring. Rifling around a pile of ashes was not what she'd pictured though. But it was just ash. Just the remains of someone long gone, and her intention was not one of disturbance or disrespect. Given Meg's help, Odette told herself that even Juleanne would understand this small intrusion. If the dead even cared about such things.

She reached her hand inside, doing her best to be sure she touched only the ring. "I'm sorry, Ms. Barbot," she whispered. Her fingers found the cool metal and she quickly pulled it free.

Once her hand was safely out of the crypt, she held the ring up and tried to blow off a little of the ash.

"Don't get that on your fancy dress," Sister Mary Cecilia said. "Let me, dearie." She took the ring and wiped it on her apron.

"No, we certainly wouldn't want to ruin that spectacular dress," a deep drawl echoed off the granite.

## CHAPTER 40

# BASTIAN

I f Bastian could feel the cold, he would have sworn a chill wind had blown into the mausoleum with Octavian's presence. The warm fire of faith and long-awaited freedom now faded to smoldering embers as he watched his old friend step through the iron doorway, brandishing a revolver.

"I'm sorry," Meg muttered from beside Octavian; her wrist gripped tight in his left hand.

"Don't snivel, sweetheart." Octavian flung the poor girl forward.

She nearly tripped over her red dress as she tumbled against the crypt. Odette and Sister Mary Cecilia helped her find her feet again.

"It's okay," Odette whispered and squeezed Meg's shaking hands. Bastian watched as she subtly stepped in front of Meg, seeming to want to keep herself between the group and Octavian's gun.

"He was going to hurt my son," Meg whimpered.

"It's okay," Bastian heard the nun softly reassuring the frightened young mother.

"You are lucky this is all turning out in my favor, or I would consider myself betrayed," Octavian said to Meg.

184

"I won't give you the ring," Odette interjected.

Bastian's chest swelled at her bravery but then dropped just as fast when he heard Octavian pull back the hammer.

"Oh, I think you will. Won't she, Bastian? Because the alternative would be rather...well...bloody. And that would certainly ruin her dress." Octavian took one step forward and pointed the muzzle toward Odette's heart.

"Give him the ring." Bastian swallowed.

"What? No!" Odette turned to him and desperately gripped his hands in her soft, cool fingers. "Bastian, we've come so close..."

Bastian brushed his thumb over hers and whispered, "I will not let him hurt you. I cannot let him hurt you." A tear burned his cheek. He felt agonized frustration at his lack of ability to physically do anything to help her. So he did the only thing he really could do; he begged. "Please, Odette...please."

"I would do what he says," Octavian said, moving closer. "Besides, I won't just hurt *you*. I will hurt all of you." He motioned the gun toward Meg and Sister Mary Cecilia.

"You are nothing but selfish," the sister spat from behind Odette, clinging to Meg's arm as the woman continued to tremble.

"And Odette isn't selfish? Bastian isn't?" Octavian laughed. "We are *all* selfish, sister. I'm just honest about it."

"Just because you believe that doesn't make it true," the nun replied with a sharp edge to her tone, her face pinched.

"I tire of this. Give me the ring. Now." Octavian trained his gun on Odette once again while holding out his free hand.

Odette's chest filled with oxygen that released in what sounded like a deep, sad sigh.

"Give it to him, my love." Bastian clasped her face in his see-through hands and pressed his lips against hers. Salty tears mixed with her sweetness.

Bastian rested his forehead against hers. He prayed for time to still, to freeze, to gift him with a few more seconds, minutes, hours with her. His last century had never seemed more wasted than in this moment before his fate was sealed for good and all hope lost.

"This is sickeningly sweet, but, again, I must insist," Octavian said, vanquishing the illusion that Bastian's request might be granted.

He watched Odette's hand stretch out, quivering, as Sister Mary Cecilia placed the ring in her palm. Her hand squeezed the small token that was the key to everything before offering it to Octavian.

The little gold trinket dropped into Octavian's hand, the rose bouncing before being wrapped in his wrinkled fingers. He held his fist against his chest and closed his eyes. "Ah," Octavian exhaled.

"Would you really do this? Relegate Bastian to an eternity cursed and alone. Your hate for him cannot be that great," Sister Mary Cecilia pleaded as she wrapped her arms around Odette, who'd stepped back weakly into her embrace.

"Perhaps not," Octavian said. "But my desire for immortality is certainly greater than any fondness I might have once had for him." He slid the ring on his finger. "I am sorry you were swept into this, Odette. I might have been fond of you as well in a different circumstance." As he spoke, the gray receded from Octavian's hair, returning to solid black, and his skin firmed with the youthful glow Bastian recognized from a time when he'd thought they had been friends.

"This isn't over," Sister Mary Cecilia said.

"I think that it is." Octavian smirked, then exited, disappearing into the foggy night.

Odette gasped.

Bastian assumed the reaction was due to Octavian's transformation until he realized her tear-filled eyes were frantically searching the mausoleum. "Odette." He reached for her, but his hand slid right through her sinew and bone, as though she wasn't there at all.

"Bastian?" Panic laced her question. "Bastian, are you still here?"

"Odette!" He shouted.

She turned her head in his direction and a slight smile broke the tension in her tear-stained face.

"He is still here," Sister Mary Cecilia said.

"Octavian didn't break the curse," Meg offered. "He just reinforced it by taking the ring for his own. Your Bastian is just pulled back closer to the veil."

"Does this mean I won't be able to see him? To hear him?" Odette looked back and forth again. "Bastian? Are you there?"

"I'm here," he said. His face was inches from hers, but her eyes stared past him. He leaned closer. "I'm here." He tried to kiss her cheek.

He felt nothing, but she touched her face, and that was something. A small glimmer of light as the world around him retreated into darkness.

"We will find another way," Sister Mary Cecilia said, holding Odette steady. Her resolve sounded unwavering, but Bastian detected doubt glistening in her gray eyes.

"I can help." Meg came to Odette's other side and held her hand.

Odette nodded. "Yes, Bastian. We will find another way. I promise, ghost-boy."

"Not a ghost," Bastian said.

Odette didn't acknowledge his routine reply. She lifted her head and inclined her ear like she was still waiting, still listening for those three words that meant nothing had changed.

"Not a ghost," Bastian repeated. Nothing. He shouted the words over and over, all without any reaction that might let him know that Odette, the nun, or Meg had heard him. Instead, Odette sobbed and crumpled to the floor. Sister Mary Cecilia and Meg knelt beside her, hugging her.

"There will be a way," Sister Mary Cecilia soothed.

*Please, God, let there be a way,* Bastian prayed to a God he had been told loved him, a God he wasn't sure he even believed in, a God who he dared to hope could hear him when no one else could. He knelt down in front of a weeping Odette, reaching to touch her but stopped short of completing the task. He felt the breaking of his own heart even more now that the miracle of touching her was gone.

His tears dripped in parallel streams, and he whispered, "I'm not a ghost."

# CHAPTER 41

# ODETTE

It was after midnight when Odette found herself back in the abbey courtyard with Sister Mary Cecilia. A thin fog crept along the ground, mingling with a light mist that had started to fall on Odette's slumped shoulders. She had pulled herself together long enough to ride the streetcar home without weeping, but the threat of returning to her sobbing was only a breath away.

She turned toward the theater, waiting for a bit of sad music to float into the night air, but there was silence. Meg said that Bastian was still there. She wanted to believe that. To hold on to the hope that she had forced on Bastian, but it waned in the shadow of her cracking heart.

"Are you alright?" Sister Mary Cecilia asked.

Odette wondered. She breathed in and out in an effort to calm her fears and tears. "I don't know, Sister. I thought I was done with love, but really I was just waiting to love someone like this, to be loved like this, and I finally have it, and it's untouchable. I feel like this is some tragic comedy and I'm the punchline."

"I am sure there will be another way." Sister Mary Cecilia touched Odette's shoulder.

Odette patted the woman's wrinkled hand but said nothing. Instead, she stared at the roses creeping up the bricks of the theater. They had gone from vibrant life to merely fading, wilting, and now dying. The crimson blooms had turned darker and hung limp against the browning leaves. She felt like those flowers.

Odette had fallen in love with Bastian Roux. It was unexpected and a bit alarming. But it was deeper than anything she had ever felt before. A see-through man, invisible to the rest of the world, had made her feel seen and safe. It was a love like she had never felt before. A love like that wakes you up to the world. It changes everything. To walk away from it, to have to live without it, was like seeing colors for the first time only to have the world fade back to gray. Odette's world was fading with the roses.

Save for one rose.

In the midst of muted reds and greens, there was one bright blossom standing in defiance. Odette moved forward toward it and reached to gingerly touch the singular lively rose. Droplets shimmered on the velvet petals. Its sweet scent whispered to Odette's senses a breath of unwavering faith.

"You think there is another way. How?" Odette turned to the nun. Her question was genuine, not a wounded retort.

"I don't know," the sister said. "But I have always said that I believe love is what breaks curses. Love will be the key." The nun took Odette's face in her worn, warm hands. Her gray eyes sparkled with confident joy. "*Love* will be the key. Somehow. Some way." She hugged Odette. "Now go rest."

Odette wiped her eyes with the back of her finger. "I don't think I can sleep. Not with..."

"Don't argue with me," Sister Mary Cecilia said with a raised brow and a pointed finger.

"I wasn't...I just..."

"Go home. Let the Maker make the plans and rest knowing that He will reveal it to you. Fretting about it all night will do nothing but drain the strength your heart needs to see this through."

"You really believe this isn't over? There's still a chance?"

"I do. And I think you do too. You just need to remind yourself of that fact." Sister Mary Cecilia hugged Odette once more. "I repeat: Go rest."

Odette nodded. She gave the red rose—which stood out like a beacon amidst the darkness—one last glance. Love will be the key. She let the phrase tumble around in her mind, praying for it to cycle into a tangible idea as she made her way home.

# CHAPTER 42
# BASTIAN

Bastian watched Odette exit through the courtyard's iron gate. He kept his eyes on her until her black dress disappeared into the night. He could still feel the specter of the fabric silky on his skin. Just a few hours before, he had held her in his arms, daring to dream that he would never have to let her go. He considered running after her, staying close to her through the night. If she could see him, though, she would probably tell him there was a fine line between haunting and stalking.

"You go rest too," Sister Mary Cecilia spoke into the vapor. "I know you are here. Go rest." She smiled and went indoors.

Bastian withdrew to the familiarity of his theatrical lair. Stepping onto the stage, it was so dark. Had it always been this dark? He'd never wished for light to bring him comfort before, but he found himself wishing for it now. Just a flicker or a flame to let him know he wasn't being swallowed by nothingness.

He spotted Odette's lantern sitting on the stage edge. He retrieved it, turning the switch. A glow grew, expanding in a circle around him. Bastian placed the light on top of his piano. He wanted to scream at the unfairness to touch the lamp, but not

Odette. This piece of his curse was a cruel injustice. Any gratitude he'd once had for fingers that could still make music had fled with Octavian. The loneliness, which had once been a small, docile creature, had grown into a ferocious dragon. Bastian sank onto the wooden floor. He wrapped his arms around his knees and dropped his head. Music would not tame the beast anyway…not tonight.

The little lamp had long since died, but dawn was breaking through covered windows. Bastian shivered. A shadow swooped past. Bastian stood up, and the floorboards creaked with the movement. Something hissed.

It circled above him, eyes flaming like hot coals.

Bastian clenched his fists and shook his head. "No, I won't give in this time." A month ago, he would have said that losing his soul was freedom because it meant a release from his constant agony of being stuck between realms. He'd felt ready for that. He would have kept begging for it all to be over. But in the wee hours of this sad morning, he still had the tiniest bit of hope swimming in his otherwise hopeless soul. He would not give in so easily. He would not let Odette carry it all on her shoulders. If he loved her, he had to fight for his own freedom.

The shadow hovered lower, until it was right in front of Bastian. He would have sworn its head tilted in examination.

"Leave me alone," Bastian quietly commanded.

The reaper inched closer and then jerked its gaze upward before hissing and fleeing into the darkness.

Bastian faltered on weak knees, catching himself with a hand against the grand piano.

"Bastian?" A whisper reverberated in his ears.

He looked up at the sound of his name—of her voice—to see Odette standing on the stage. Her normally bright eyes were bloodshot and puffy behind her glasses. Her hair and clothes were a bit disheveled. The previous night, she'd shone and sparkled with life. Now, pale and timid, she seemed to be the ghost.

"Odette."

She showed no sign of having heard him but continued to search through the room with her eyes, "I wish I could see you."

"I'm right here." He stepped close to her, his body barely brushing against hers.

"I hope you are here, otherwise I have really lost my mind and am just talking to myself in an abandoned building."

"I'm here," Bastian whispered into her ear, but again, she gave no inclination that she could hear or feel him. He needed to do something. Find a way to let her know he was there.

*The music.*

Bastian sat down on the piano bench and lifted the lid. He played three notes.

"Bastian." Odette turned with a smile that lit the entire stage and Bastian's spirit.

He made room for her as she sat down on the bench. He played two more shaky notes.

Odette blew out a waiting breath and smiled again. "I needed to talk to you, to tell you…"

Bastian's heart thumped like a bass drum and he played C, then B.

"I love you," she said.

"I love you," he replied with a D, E, and F.

"I should have told you before. I need you to know I mean it with my whole heart." Odette fidgeted with a piece of her wavy hair. "I don't want to live without you, Bas."

Bastian's fingers trickled along the keyboard in a soft melody that matched his soaring emotions. He didn't want to live without her. But…he hit a minor chord. "I don't want to be your prison."

Odette bit her lip. "I wish I could at least hear your voice." A tear escaped from the corner of her eye and slid to her lips. She wiped it away with the back of her hand. "I know you want to debate this, ghost-boy…"

Bastian played three quick notes. "Not a ghost."

Odette giggled, then turned to face him. "I still have hope. And I would rather have you in part than not at all."

Bastian felt his breath catch at her in-between eyes—dancing between colors like the first time he'd seen them—glistening and deep and inviting him in. He pressed a single ivory key, holding it down.

Odette placed her hand on the spot as the sound faded. It slipped through Bastian's, but he didn't move as this piece of him intertwined with this piece of her. "I will love you my whole life."

"I will love you for my eternity."

Neither spoke nor moved. The space between them was electric with anticipation. Bastian's heart beat loud in his ears, thumping to the rhythm of Odette's increasingly rapid breaths. Her brow furrowed and her bottom lip quivered. She bit it. A stream of tears broke loose from her searching eyes.

"It didn't work. It wasn't enough," she muttered. "She said love was the key, and I thought…" She stood up.

Bastian reached for her arm, but his fingers slipped right through. "Odette, it's ok…" He played the intro to a love song.

"No!" Odette shouted, and Bastian stopped his melody. "It didn't work," she cried. Her fingers twisted the hem of her sweater. She stood fragile in the dim morning sunbeams that were able to make their way to the platform. "I'm sorry," her voice shook.

"Odette." Bastian knocked the piano bench as he stood.

But she still couldn't hear him. She still couldn't see him. And she was gone again.

# CHAPTER 43
# ODETTE

Odette slammed the theater door shut and then leaned against it. She blinked away the ever-brighter morning sun which glared through her tear-stained eyes. Her chest heaved with sobs, but mostly frustration. What had made her so sure her confession would work? She had been naive to think fairytales could come true and curses could be broken.

"What's the matter, dearie?" Sister Mary Cecilia asked from her potting bench, a spade in one hand and dark brown soil smeared on her cheek and apron. Was she always up this early or had sleep evaded her as well?

"It didn't work. Love is not enough." Odette nearly choked on the words.

"What do you mean? Tell me exactly what has happened." Sister Mary Cecilia gestured for Odette to come sit at the small bistro table on the patio.

The metal seat was cold and a little damp. "So, I told Bastian how much I loved him, that I would love him for my whole life. I thought…I thought…I don't know what I thought, but…"

"You thought your admission would break the curse."

"Well, yes." Odette fixed her gaze on her lap. "You said love was the key."

Sister Mary Cecilia huffed. Loudly. "This generation is so hung up on romantic gestures and platitudes...I blame movies." She chuckled and then regained her stern composure. "When I said love was the key, I meant real love. The *agape* kind."

"I don't understand," Odette sniffled. She used her sleeve to wipe her face.

"I can see that." She removed her gardening gloves and folded her hands together on the table. "We are all under a curse and the only thing that has ever been able to break it has been love. But not the kind found in words and kisses. That stuff is for stories. This kind of love is not so much a feeling—it's not butterflies in your stomach—it's sacrifice. It's humility and forgiveness and putting the needs of others above ourselves. It's the kind of love that doesn't always feel good and isn't always convenient. It's a love that transforms and longs to be shared." The nun paused and held out her hand to Odette.

Odette took the offer. As Sister Mary Cecilia's fingers wrapped around hers, the tremble under her skin subsided.

"My dear, true—I mean really true love—isn't found in a confession or a kiss...it's found in a choice."

Sparks popped into Odette's spirit. "Breaking this curse isn't just about choosing Bastian, is it?"

"No, I'm afraid that is only part of it," Sister Mary Cecilia said. "It's about wanting something for him more than for yourself. It's about loving him beyond yourself. It's about being a bridge that leads him to the only love that is truly enough."

Odette's lungs filled with the chilly morning air and understanding. "I get it now. And I think I know what I have to do."

"Are you sure?"

"I'm not the type to just let things go."

"No, you are not." Sister Mary Cecilia released Odette's hand with a pat and a grin.

"I have a phone call to make."

The two ladies stood.

Odette paused. "You've always known the key, haven't you?"

"Maybe," Sister Mary Cecilia said.

"Why not tell me sooner? Why let me do all the searching in all the wrong places?"

"The search is part of the journey. You needed it for this to be real." The nun put her gloves back on. "One last thing," she said. "You aren't alone. You've never been alone." Her eyes tilted ever-so-slightly upward.

"I know."

# CHAPTER 44
# OCTAVIAN

Octavian had his bag packed and a car scheduled to pick him up for the airport in a matter of moments. He'd head back to Rome to finish his business there now that his business in New Orleans was eternally complete.

He turned Bastian's ring on his smooth finger. His wrinkles had vanished and his muscles had felt rejuvenated the moment he had slid it on his hand. He'd slept better last night than he had in days, waking without even the hint of a backache.

Octavian checked the time on his pocket watch. It was wonderfully, silently stopped at eleven thirteen and eight seconds. "All is as it should be." He clapped it shut, running his finger over the serpent design before placing it back in his jacket pocket.

Just as his phone dinged a notification that his driver had arrived, a folded piece of paper slipped under his room's door. He was tempted to ignore it and leave it behind with every other memory of this city, but a sudden curiosity outweighed his eagerness to leave.

Unfolding it, scribbled in blue ink, he read,

*I have a proposal for you. Please meet me at the theater.*

*Odette*

As soon as her name breached his lips, a click echoed inside his breast pocket. "No," he hissed.

Another tick was followed by another and another.

Octavian glanced at his reflection in the wall mirror. "How?" As quickly as it had faded in the crypt's dull light, the gray had streaked back into his hair. It was just the gray. No other signs of age yet marred his features. For that, he was thankful. Nonetheless, he was enraged.

For one hundred years, he had moved around in this world untouched by its mortality. He had tricked the powers-that-be of their rule over him. They would no longer write his fate, he had taken control and written it himself. Or so he had thought…until Odette. But he would not be undone by some foolish girl and her notions of romance. Octavian did not believe in fairytales, but he would become the villain of this one if he had to. He would meet her at the Castle Rose and end this once and for all. He would seal the curse in blood…her blood.

# CHAPTER 45
# ODETTE

Odette stepped out onto the stage and couldn't help but think about soloists and grand finales. Did their palms get clammy too? She wiped hers on her jeans and pushed her glasses up her nose.

Soft notes fluttered toward her.

Odette smiled. "I'm sorry about before. For walking out. I…"

Another string of music danced into her ears.

Odette was about to explain herself, to divulge her new plan, but before she could muster the courage to tell Bastian what she was about to do, the tattered curtain ruffled.

Octavian pushed aside the heavy fabric with a cough and a wave of his hand to push away the flurry of released dust.

"You got my message," Odette said. Her insides tingled as she clenched her fists.

"I did." Octavian adjusted the cuffs of his jacket. "I'm not sure what you could possibly have to offer me, but I was intrigued." He pulled a gold watch from inside his jacket and sneered before returning it. "Though I'm afraid we don't have much time. I have a flight to catch."

Minor chords banged. The piano bench creaked.

Odette glanced toward Bastian's invisible presence. If there was ever a time in her life to be courageous, it was now. She inhaled a bitter breath and exhaled her resolve, turning her attention squarely to Octavian. "I asked you here to offer myself."

More low notes pounded into the air. "What? No!" Bastian shouted.

Odette's gaze jerked back toward Bastian who was now emerging from oblivion—faint but visible. "Bas?" Odette couldn't help the grin that spread across her face and the jolt of electricity speeding up her heartbeat.

"Yourself?" Octavian asked, seeming to ignore their interaction, although Odette felt she could detect a tinge of fear creeping through his outwardly calm demeanor at Bastian's reemergence. He stepped closer to Odette, floorboards squeaking with the movement.

"Yes." Odette straightened her shoulders. "Set Bastian free in exchange for me being tethered to your immortality. Meg said it was possible if…"

"You would take his place?" Octavian raised an eyebrow. His mouth twisted in disgust.

"Yes," Odette replied.

"No, Odette." Bastian rushed to her side and took her hand in his. "You can't do this."

Odette looked down at her hand. Her grin widened. She laced her fingers with his. "You are worthy of love."

"I didn't understand it before." Tears snuck from the corners of Bastian's gray eyes. "But I do now. I've learned real love and where I once would have let someone take my place. I can't now. I won't be selfish again."

Odette wiped his damp cheek with her thumb. "You are not *letting* me do anything. This is not selfish. This is so far from self-ishness and pride and fear." Her fingers played with a lock of his curly hair, then settled on the back of his neck. "This is freedom for both of us. I would gladly give myself so that you might have a chance to live."

Bastian wrapped his hand around hers. "You have already

shown me real love and life. It is enough to feed my soul for an eternity." Bastian leaned forward and offered a small, sweet kiss.

"But it isn't about *my* love, Bas." Odette stared into his see-through eyes, searching for acknowledgment and understanding. This couldn't be about her. It wasn't about her. It wasn't about some haunted romance. That's not the kind of love that breaks curses.

Bastian's lip curled upward just a touch. "I know," he whispered.

"No," Octavian stated.

A shadow moved overhead.

"What?" Odette asked. "Why not? You still get what you want."

"That's where you are wrong." Octavian pulled his revolver from a holster inside his jacket and checked that it was fully loaded. "Your nauseating confessions of love tell me that if either of you is allowed freedom, you will simply use it in attempts to save each other—over and over again for an eternity." He spun the gun's cylinder and clicked it back into place. "I simply cannot risk that." He aimed at Odette.

"We won't. You have our word," Odette said, ignoring the tremble that quaked through her body.

"Your word means nothing to me," Octavian said, his thumb resting on the hammer.

Odette winced, then shivered as the shadow passed again. A rotten smell burned her nose. This wasn't a play of the light; something truly dark was there with them. Was it there for Bastian? Fear nudged and poked at her confidence. Was death waiting in the wings to take him? To take her?

*You are not alone.* The nun's words whispered through Odette's thoughts. They mingled with truths planted in her heart and now sprouting to life. She need not be afraid because perfect love casts out fear. She would not be afraid.

"Take us both, then," Odette offered. She slowly removed her grandmother's turquoise ring. "Take my ring too. Meg said it will bind me to you just like Bastian's did for him." She set the band on the top of the piano next to the nun's crystal vase holding a single red rose; the last thriving rose.

Octavian eyed the piece of silver jewelry. "To what end?" He lowered the revolver a touch, but a wicked grin spread over his face and darkened his eyes.

"Two souls tethered to yours means more power for you," Odette said.

"You can't be sure of that. But I can be sure it will give you two some semblance of a ghostly happily-ever-after. Why would I do that?" Octavian sniggered.

The shadow hovered over the piano and hissed.

"I don't know. Because you aren't completely awful. Because you have a heart. Because love breeds hope, and we can hope you will do something the tiniest bit benevolent," Odette said.

"Love is a trick," Octavian scorned.

"No," Bastian said, turning to offer Odette a brief smile before looking back to Octavian. "Love is no trick. It is the answer to every hole you have ever tried to fill." He took two steps forward.

"Watch yourself, friend," Octavian hissed the endearment. "I will kill her." Octavian raised his gun again.

Odette flinched and then watched the shadow lower itself as it floated round and round the trio. Darkness took the form of a wispy apparition. Her skin prickled as its eyes surveyed them. Red embers glared from one to the other and then settled on Octavian, flaming brighter as it drew close to him. Did Octavian see it? If so, he gave no inclination or acknowledgment of its dastardly presence. But it saw him. Whatever this thing was, Odette surmised it was not good. It was not from the Maker. It wanted Octavian Zane.

Octavian retrieved Odette's ring, studying it. "You want me to believe that love conquers all, is that it? Bah! We shall see if your love holds any kind of power when you watch her die." He put a finger to the trigger.

"And you think power conquers?" Bastian stepped back in front of Odette.

She had to peer around him, as his form became no longer see-through at all.

"It has conquered my death," Octavian retorted.

"No, death circles you even now," Bastian said as his head turned up to look at the shadow.

Octavian looked up. His eyes darted back and forth but locked onto nothing. "You lie." He squeezed the revolver's grip tighter. His skin wrinkled and dulled. Grey began to pepper his black hair.

"He who conquers must first conquer himself," Bastian said. "And the only thing that has conquered all my insecurities and shame has been Love itself."

Octavian held the gun up with a shaking hand. "Love is weak," he said with a tremor in his voice.

"No, it isn't," Odette said, stepping out beside Bastian and reaching for his hand before looking back at Octavian, her determination in the truth of their message emboldening her.

The shadowed figure floated in front of Octavian. It lifted a gangly finger and scratched a line along his sternum.

Octavian gripped his chest as though something had stopped his heart and squeezed his lungs. He dropped the gun.

Bang!

Odette clutched Bastian, burying her face in his shoulder. She held her breath, waiting for pain or blood, but there was none. The accidental shot had missed. She peeked out and saw Octavian reaching for the piano in an attempt to hold himself upright.

He glared at his age-spotted hands.

The shadow watched him, its fiery eyes seeming to dance like flames, wicked with delight.

"This doesn't have to be your end," Bastian said.

"He's right," Odette said as she stepped forward toward the piano. Octavian may be a villainous beast, Odette thought, but he deserved a chance at mercy just as much as Bastian, as her, as anyone. Just days ago, she would have wished him the same despair he had caused; but seeing that dark vulture circle him again stoked compassion she didn't realize she possessed. She gently touched Octavian's arm. "You never needed immortality…not like this…Love was enough for Bastian, and it can be for you. You just have to accept it…accept your need for it."

Octavian pulled away from her and pushed himself to stand. He wobbled and his breath came in heaves. "And be chained to another's will?" He grimaced.

"There are no chains with this love." Bastian offered Octavian a hand.

Odette's breath caught. Bastian stood, hand outstretched in an offering of grace, his body full and bright with life. His eyes sparkled and his curls glossed even in the faint lighting of the dilapidated theater. His cheeks were flushed with life.

"This…isn't…possible…" Octavian huffed through broken breaths.

The dark creature crept closer and closer to Zane.

"You're running out of time, old friend," Bastian said.

"We were never friends," Octavian choked out.

"We could be," Bastian replied.

Octavian clung to Odette's ring as the color drained from his face. His eyes widened as he stared into the flaming eyes of his demise. His chin trembled. The shadow wrapped a smoky hand around his throat. "But I have the key." His words gurgled in his throat as he lowered to his knees.

"No, you don't," Bastian whispered.

The shadow covered the aging, dying man like a blanket. It shrieked and screamed as it consumed him, then disappeared, along with all traces of Octavian Zane.

Odette covered her mouth.

Bastian's eyes were glassy with puddled tears. "That could have been me. So many times, that reaper hovered near to me. It could've been me."

"But it wasn't," Odette said. She stepped close to him, tucking herself under his arm and nestling into his shoulder. There was no cool chill. No charge of static. Only a flood of gratitude washing over her.

Bastian rested his cheek against her head. "It didn't have to be him."

"No, it didn't," Odette said. A warm tear slid down her cheek. What would it have taken for a man like Zane to have made a different choice? What had broken inside him and filled him with such hate that he would shun love? Odette wondered if she'd had those answers, perhaps Bastian wouldn't have been the only one saved here. But you can't force someone to open their eyes or their heart. You can only offer them the key and let them choose for themselves.

A shimmer caught Odette's eye and broke her mulling. Their two rings lay on the dusty floor. Odette pulled away, then bent down and picked them up. "I believe this is yours." She handed Bastian his grandfather's rose signet ring.

"It was just a ring," he whispered.

"Now it can be a reminder," Odette said.

"Of love?" He slid it onto his finger.

Odette returned her ring to her hand. "That we have already been conquered."

# CHAPTER 46
# BASTIAN

Bastian Roux stepped out of the Castle Rose and for the first time in one hundred years, he felt the sun warm on his skin and the air fresh and cool in his lungs. The door closed behind him, the door of his prison, the door of his curse. He was walking into freedom and was both elated and anxious. This was his second chance, but it would require learning to live again.

"Bastian!" Sister Mary Cecilia gasped and dropped the flowerpot in her hand, sending it crashing onto the patio bricks. She bustled toward him and bound him in a tight embrace.

Her joyous tears soaked through his cotton shirt. "Yes, Sister. It's me."

She pulled away and grabbed his chin, turning his face back and forth so she could study it. "Look at you," she said. "Look at *me* looking *at* you," she laughed. She let go of him and wiped her wet face with her gloved hands, leaving her usual smear of dirt behind. "It is a miracle." She turned to Odette and pointed her finger. "I told you love was the key."

"That you did, Sister." Odette's smile was wide. It lit her entire countenance in a way that made Bastian feel brave enough to take on this new world. "Thank you," she said, hugging the nun.

"It was just a little guidance," she grinned. "We are all just the bridges, after all." Sister Mary Cecilia stepped backward and smoothed her apron, then looked back and forth between Bastian and Odette. "What now?"

*What now?* That hadn't been a question Bastian had needed to answer in decades. For the first time in a very long time, his answer would matter. It could make a mark on the world. There could be purpose in it. There *was* purpose in it. He felt like he was walking to the edge of the water and deciding whether to dive straight into the deep end, only he didn't even know what the deep end was. But he could wade into the shallows one step at a time.

"Well," he said, "it has always been my habit to ride the trolley each morning and take in the beauty of this city."

"Then let's do that." Odette curled her arm around his. "But first, let's get coffee. Huge cups of coffee."

Bastian laughed. "And beignets. I have craved a good beignet."

"Definitely beignets. And I know the best in the city." Odette kissed his cheek. "Oh, Lizzie is going to love you. And you better love her. She's family." She tugged him forward, past the lush blooms of the rose wall, through the garden gate, and out onto the street toward Madame Clary's and toward a new life.

# CODA: BASTIAN, 2024

Chatter filled the cozy room. Bastian rubbed his hands together and stretched his fingers. He blinked, adjusting his eyes to the two spotlights which illuminated the small stage. It was barely big enough for the baby grand piano where he sat. He inhaled, filling his lungs to capacity before exhaling slowly.

His eyes scanned the crowd until he found Odette.

She sat at a cafe table, front and center, chatting with Isabelle. Her eyes sparkled as she laughed at something the old woman had said. When Lizzie and Joe entered with Sister Mary Cecilia, she waved them over to the table next to her. After a quick hug and a sip of her coffee, she seemed to resettle and then met his gaze.

Her lips curved into the smile he treasured more than his own happiness. She waved delicate fingers and mouthed, *"You're going to be great."*

Bastian winked. He ran his hand through his hair and took another deep breath.

His heart fluttered, and his knee bobbed.

Was he nervous?

He had played on larger stages for larger crowds. He had

played for much higher stakes than a coffee house open mic night. He should be well past stage fright.

But this was different.

This was brand new.

He was brand new.

Once upon a time, the Maker had given him a gift. Music had enchanted him. His music had enchanted others. He hadn't realized then how he'd used this gift only for his own purposes. He'd made himself the center of it all, thinking that would bring him fulfillment. All the validation and applause the world offered had not been enough to fill the hunger of his soul. He hadn't seen it before; how corrupted and skewed his path had become.

He saw it now.

He saw himself now—fully and completely—his gifts and his flaws.

A voice whispered that he would make the same mistakes, that he would fall into the same traps.

Bastian looked at the ring on his right hand.

He turned it until the rose lined up with his knuckle and, as it did, it was as if his heart aligned with peace.

Love had consumed and conquered; it had filled his weak places. He was no longer his own and no longer on his own. He was not the center, even of his own life, and that acknowledgment brought a strange sense of freedom.

Bastian touched deft fingers to the ivory keys. Five short notes floated above the hum of activity, bringing it to a halt.

"I love you," Bastian whispered to a watching and waiting Odette.

Then he played a new song.

# ACKNOWLEDGMENTS

I cannot count how many cups of coffee it took to write this story. And don't ask me how many times each cup was reheated. Let's just say I should probably have superpowers by now from the mix of caffeine and microwave radiation. (I may be slightly disappointed that I don't.) In my experience, writing a book takes a lot of coffee…and a lot of support. I *can* count the people to whom I owe a debt of gratitude.

My husband, Brian, has kept me in lattes, chocolate, and hugs. I am thankful he exists. I am thankful I get to do life with him. I am thankful that his crazy matches my crazy. He is forever my favorite person.

My daughters, Lila and Lorelai, make me feel smarter, cooler, and more heroic than I actually am. I am thankful for their hugs, witty humor, and random outbursts of Hamilton lyrics. I am so proud to be their mom.

My publishing team at Blue Ink Press keeps me grounded. I am thankful to Sherry, Amanda, & Stephanie for continuing to invest in me and my stories. I don't know what I'd do without my editors, Liz and Christa, for making this story shine and dealing with my complete lack of regard for the proper usage of commas.

My friends are the best! Aly, Laura, Vanessa, Emerald, Victoria, and so many more have been my relentless supporters. I am thankful for every text, message, and moment of encouragement. They have all taught me that writing does not have to be lonely work.

My street team rocks all of the socks! I am thankful for each moment they gift me with their enthusiasm, time, and energy to share my stories with the world. I wish I could send you all beignets!

My readers, I am thankful for you. I am always humbled that you would choose to pick up one of my books. I am thankful for your time and for every kind word and review. I hope you found hope, purpose, and a little joy in these pages.

My gracious Maker. He has carried me and conquered me. I am thankful to serve a God who is love, and whose love for me is deep and wide and infinite. I am thankful for it and for the chance to be a bridge so others might experience it.

# ABOUT THE AUTHOR

Tabitha Caplinger gets way too emotionally invested in the lives of fictional characters, whether it's obsessing over a book or tv show, or getting lost creating her own worlds. Tabitha is the author of Christian fantasy such as The Wolf Queen and The Chronicle of the Three Trilogy, and a lover of good stories and helping others live chosen. When she's not writing book words, she's reheating her coffee, binging a new show or teaching God's Word to young adults. Tabitha, her husband and two beautifully sassy daughters desire to be Jesus with skin on for those around them. They live to love others...and for Marvel movies.

www.ingramcontent.com/pod-product-compliance
Lightning Source LLC
Chambersburg PA
CBHW031445200726

48289CB00007BB/2276